STRIKE THREE, YOU'RE DEAD

LENNY & THE MIKES

JOSH BERK

ALFRED A. KNOPF

NEW YORK

THIS IS A BORZOI BOOK PUBLISHED BY ALFRED A. KNOPF

Visit us on the Web! randomhouse.com/kids

Educators and librarians, for a variety of teaching tools,
visit us at RHTeachersLibrarians.com

Library of Congress Cataloging-in-Publication Data
Berk, Josh.
Strike three, you're dead / Josh Berk.
p. cm.
Summary: Lenny Norbeck and his friends The Mikes set out to investigate
the suspicious death of a young pitcher at a Phillies game.
ISBN 978-0-375-87008-8 (trade) — ISBN 978-0-375-97008-5 (lib. bdg.) —
ISBN 978-0-375-98736-6 (ebook)
[1. Baseball—Fiction. 2. Murder—Fiction. 3. Best friends—Fiction.
4. Friendship—Fiction. 5. Philadelphia Phillies (Baseball team)—Fiction.
6. Mystery and detective stories.] I. Title. II. Title: Strike three, you are dead.
PZ7.B452295Str 2013
[Fic]—dc23
2012023892

The text of this book is set in 12.5-point Goudy.

Printed in the United States of America

March 2013

10 9 8 7 6 5 4 3

First Edition

This book is dedicated to my family, with all the love in the world (even the one of you who is a Yankees fan).

PROLOGUE

"No one gets killed in the suburbs."

I say this out loud, more to myself than anyone else. I keep saying it. Over and over, like the words might form a shield to protect me. "No one gets killed in the suburbs. No one gets killed in the suburbs." I'm trying to convince myself. I'm not doing such a good job, though. I'm hard to convince.

I crouch down farther, trying to make myself as small as possible. I bury my face in my chest, wrapping myself in my arms and legs like I'm a big human fist. The shed we're behind is dirty and it smells. It's also in the backyard of a murderer.

What were we thinking?

Mike is talking out loud too, also muttering to no one in particular. "I promise I'll give my baseball card collection to poor children if we get out of here alive," he says. He looks up at the sky. Maybe he *is* talking to someone in particular.

Other Mike joins in. "I'll give my computer to poor children." He is terrified. His pale skin is even whiter than usual. He looks like he saw a ghost—no, he looks like he *is* a ghost.

Mike takes it a step further. "If we get out of this, I'll be nice to my sister," he whispers. "Forever."

Now I know he's really scared. This is serious.

I don't have a sister and I can't think of anything really valuable I own to give to poor children. Plus, I'm not actually convinced that promising to give your stuff away will save you at a time like this. I do have one thing I want to promise, though. So I say that to Mike. I apologize. And I mean it. He mutters, "Thanks." And that's that.

I just keep repeating my belief that nothing sinister ever happens around here. It's true, more or less. Serious crime in Schwenkfelder, Pennsylvania, is when someone's horse jumps a fence and runs whinnying through the neighbor's yard. Or when someone's teenager jumps a fence and runs whinnying through the neighbor's yard. Nothing major. Yet here me and the Mikes are, crouched in the mud behind a dirty shed, bargaining for our lives. All because of some stupid contest. All because I felt bad for some dead baseball player and had to go around playing detective. Now look where it's gotten me: practically dead myself. It's just a matter of minutes—no, seconds—before my entire life is over.

"Just to let you know," Mike whispers without looking at me. "If we hear a gunshot, it's every man for himself. I'm booking it and not looking back."

"That's ridiculous," I whisper, again trying to convince myself. "We're not going to hear a gunshot. That's a bluff."

He raises his eyebrows.

We all hold our breath, waiting to see what will happen next. The sound of twigs crunching under someone's feet nearly makes me jump. A few seconds later, a loud blast shatters the suburban quiet. But the noise is not from a gun. It's from a bomb.

CHAPTER ONE

"Enter the Armchair Announcer contest today! You could be in the booth!" boomed legendary broadcaster Buck Foltz. In this commercial, as always, Buck was wearing a bright maroon blazer. His toupee seemed even more unbelievable than normal. His man-wig made it look like a small woodland creature was perching on his head. I expected it to hop up and scurry away at any moment. Oh, Buck. (What kind of a name is *Buck*, anyway? Is *Buck* short for something? What? Buckathan? Buck-ua? Buck-ard?)

Everything about the commercial was cheesier than a cheesesteak with extra cheese. The contest it was advertising was pretty cool, though. You'd submit a video of yourself being an announcer, and then one "Armchair Announcer" would be picked as winner and get to be a broadcaster for one inning of a live Phillies game. Who wouldn't want that? Isn't that everyone's dream? Well, maybe not *everyone*. Maybe some people want to be president or an astronaut or whatever. And, okay, yeah, walking on the moon would be fun. I *get* that. But, to me, announcing an inning of a Phils game was the coolest thing I could imagine. It's my dream job—baseball announcer. You get to travel with the team, be on TV, and basically get paid to watch baseball.

Best job ever.

My best friends, Mike and Other Mike, flipped out the first time we saw the commercial for the contest. We were watching baseball out on the lawn behind Mike's house. (Mike's dad installed a long cable extension so we could watch TV outside because he is the coolest dad ever.) When I say the Mikes flipped out, I mean *all the way out*. They were jumping around, immediately demanding that I enter. I wanted to do it, yeah, but I felt a little scared. Sure, I was a good announcer. I was always pretending it was my job to announce day-to-day life. And I was good at baseball too. I did a great Buck Foltz impression. I was the king of cracking the Mikes up on the lawn couch. But they were sort of an easy audience. Did I really have the skills for an audience larger than two?

"Are you thinking what I'm thinking?" Mike said to Other Mike.

"That this is a perfect opportunity to bust out my new digital video camera and fire up the killer editing suite on my new computer?" Other Mike said. He was so excited that he jumped in the air, flailing his skinny arms. His messy blond hair fell over his eyes. He looked like a baby bird attempting flight. He *always* made me think of a baby bird. Other Mike was a constant twitch. His clothes never seemed to fit right. He was constantly tugging at his belt, his sleeves, the neck of his shirt, adjusting and readjusting but never, ever getting it right.

"No," said Mike. "I mean that if our Leonard here wins, maybe we'll all get to meet Famosa!"

Phillies catcher Ramon Famosa was our favorite player for the following reasons: (1) he had an enormous and hilarious mustache that curled at both ends, and (2) he didn't speak English, so he had to travel with his father, who served as an interpreter. His dad was a tiny man known as Don Guardo who always wore crazy clothes and funny hats. That was all it took. Famosa wasn't even that great and was mainly getting playing time because of a bunch of injuries. But we loved him. Some guys liked the star sluggers, and some guys liked the strong-armed, fireballing pitchers. We liked those guys too, sure, but we *really* liked the weirdos. There are lots of oddballs in baseball, the kind of players Buck was always calling "real characters." Those characters are one of the reasons baseball is such a great game. There are lots of them throughout the game's history, and I'm kind of an expert.

There was the "Mad Hungarian," Al Hrabosky, who used to talk to baseballs. Out loud. During games. Plus, he had a great mustache. Then there was Bill Lee, the pitcher known as "Spaceman," who was always saying crazy stuff, like how he wanted to paint the White House pink and turn it into a Mexican restaurant. And he had an awesome beard. And no, we weren't just fans of facial hair. We liked historical weirdos too, like Dizzy Dean, Daffy Dean, and Yogi Berra. We liked to read about Rube Waddell, who did cartwheels on his way off the mound and sometimes would chase fire trucks during games. I loved a really old player named Rabbit Maranville, who once punched an umpire.

Famosa was the closest thing the Phils had to a classic oddball. Don Guardo seemed really funny, and, yes, the mustache was great. Famosa wasn't a great (or even very good) catcher, but we were fans for life.

Okay, when I say "we," I mainly mean "me and Mike." Other Mike barely cared about baseball, to be honest. He was way more excited about his computer than about the Phillies. "I can get my mom to go to Best Buy for a new shock-mounted condenser microphone, and maybe we can do some animated visuals. There's no way we'll lose!"

"What do you two mean," I asked in a fancy announcer voice, "when you say *we* will get to meet Famosa or that *we* will win this contest? Surely you are forgetting that I am Lenny, the boy with the golden voice!" I made my vocal cords boom just like Buck Foltz's did. I don't know if there is really anything special about my voice or if the Mikes are just easily amused. But they sometimes call me the "boy with the golden voice" because I'm good at impressions. The "boy with the golden voice" wasn't too bad as far as nicknames go. In middle school, there were a lot worse. Take, for example, Stephen Farsnickle, who absolutely everyone called "Stevie Fart-Sniffer." It was kinda his fault, though. I mean, if your last name was already Farsnickle, why would you admit that you liked smelling your own gas?

"You'll be Lenny, the boy with no friends, if you keep that up," Other Mike said.

"You'll be the boy with no butt if you keep that up," Mike said. "Because I'll kick it right off you if you get to hang with Famosa and don't bring us." Mike was shorter than me, but a hundred times stronger. He probably could literally kick off a guy's butt if he wanted to.

"All right," I said. "We're in it to win it. Team effort, as always." Seeing the excited looks on their faces made me think maybe I could really do it. Maybe I *could* win the Armchair Announcer contest. With the Mikes in my corner, I felt like I at least had a chance. Without them, I wouldn't have even tried.

And, yeah, I know it is a little confusing having two best friends named Mike, so here's what you need to know: Mike was small and solid, built like a bulldog. Baseball fanatic, snack-food enthusiast. Other Mike was half a foot taller, yet they weighed exactly the same. Tall and skinny, Other Mike was always bouncing around like an uncoiled spring. He loved computers and warlocks. Yes, warlocks. Don't ask *me*. He moved into the neighborhood last, so even though he was three months older, he was "Other Mike." He kept hoping he'd get a cool new nickname once we left elementary school, but after one year of middle school, he was still "Other Mike." It showed no signs of stopping. He'll probably be Other Mike forever. His wife will probably call him "Other Mike" (in the unlikely event someone will want to marry him). Someday his driver's license will say "Other Mike." His grandkids will probably call him "Grandpa Other Mike."

We attempted a high five out there near the lawn couch, but our hands connected with only air; somehow we smacked each other in the head and all ended up in the grass. Other Mike's glasses were nearly broken, a knee found my groin, and Mike's thumb was wrenched backward. I felt bad—he was already trying to recover from an arm injury that had ended his career as a promising pitcher at a young age. That's why we were both just fans, not players. Why wasn't I, Lenny Norbeck, a member of the baseball team? I'm glad you asked. Actually, I'm *not* glad you asked. It's a long and embarrassing tale. Let's just say this: I did play once, and I was the worst there ever was. . . .

The failed high five hurt, but I found myself smiling as I grimaced on the scratchy grass watching the clouds darken and gather. The summer suddenly seemed a bit more exciting. It was, to tell you the truth, looking like a whole lot of nothing for a while there. The Mikes and I used to go to Happy Paddler summer camp every year, but we decided against it this year. Actually, *they* decided against it this year. I *liked* Happy Paddler. But the Mikes said it was "too babyish," and I wasn't about to disagree. So what was I going to do all summer? The Norbecks weren't planning any exciting vacations. My parents would be working at the hospital all the time, like always. They're both cardiologists—heart doctors—which isn't as exciting as it sounds. Maybe it doesn't even sound exciting.

Mom's big plan for me over the summer was "early enrichment classes" at a local college. A college! I'm twelve! And I got a D in sixth-grade science! I'm not going to be a doctor! Still, Mom threw the brochure on the table on the last day of school and said, "Let me know which class you want to take." The choices were in two categories: "the arts" and "the smarts." My answer of "I'll take the farts" did not exactly sit well. Shocking, I know. But I did *not* want to study painting or pottery and certainly did not want anything to do with the smarts category. The feeling was probably mutual.

I was pretty sure Mom was dead set on making me go, but then I had a genius idea. I told her she could save money by letting me just run my own enrichment program. I told her the Schwenkfelder Public Library had a summer reading club, which was true. I also told her I was going to make it my personal mission to break the record for most books read during a single summer. That was a stretch, but it seemed to appease her for a bit, even though the record is about two hundred books, and I'm not sure they have that many baseball books, so I probably won't get close. I was mainly just hoping she'd drop the "enrichment" thing. Seriously, what kind of twelve-year-old is preparing for college? Arts, smarts, farts.

So with the parents working all the time and no camp for this guy, Who was watching Lenny? you might ask. The answer to that was: Courtney DeLuca. Courtney was the twenty-one-year-old daughter of one of Dad's doctor friends home on break from Villanova University. She was very tan and very short, with a soaring hairstyle that she apparently thought made her look taller. Mom and Dad tried to explain that Courtney was a "caretaker," there to "watch the house." Yeah, right. I knew who she was. A *babysitter*. Too old for summer camp, but I still needed a babysitter? The thought sort of made me want to puke. Between that and my ridiculous claim that I would read two hundred books, this was clearly going to be the worst summer ever.

But now this? Armchair Announcer? Could I really do it? I would love it. For once I wouldn't be just watching baseball on TV—I'd be there under the bright lights myself. I'd be there at the ballpark, rubbing shoulders with the pros. I'd be the star, and everyone would be cheering for *me*. Ever since middle school started, I'd been feeling like, What's *my* thing, you know? I wasn't tall or handsome or extraordinary. I wasn't a sports star, I wasn't getting all A's like the smart kids. I was just . . . Lenny. Mom and Dad might not think baseball announcer is a real career goal, but maybe it's my thing! If I win this contest, they would have to take off work to at least come see it. Right? Right. Everyone would have to notice. Lenny Norbeck, star announcer. I liked the sound of that.

Of course, I had no idea that the contest was just the pregame warm-up. The summer's main event would be murder. Literally.

CHAPTER TWO

Entering the Armchair Announcer contest seemed like it would be easy enough, even though I was grounded from the computer at home. It was my punishment for getting that D in science class. If your parents are doctors and you almost fail science, it looks bad. It's not my fault that Mrs. Rhodes was the meanest teacher ever. All that kingdom, phylum, class, order, family, genus stuff was impossible. I'm not even sure *phylum* is a real word. Sounds made-up. Computer grounding had been the threat all year. I didn't think they meant it. But they did. I got a D, and so it was a summer-long grounding from the PC for me. Harsh.

So I used the computer at Other Mike's house and logged on to the Phillies website. He had an awesome computer. It was superfast. You just had to check a box on the site that said you had parental consent. Easy enough. Did any kid ever check "No, my parents aren't letting me do this"? I knew I should have asked Mom and Dad, but I didn't feel like it. Mom and Dad weren't exactly baseball fans. Plus, neither of them would have loved the idea of having to drive me into Philadelphia to announce an inning, even if it was my great dream. We lived in a suburb just a few miles outside the city, but they always acted like driving to the ballpark was a trip to the moon. I know, I know, busy parents, lonely kid. Poor me. Wah-wah.

"Okay, okay, okay," Other Mike started, getting up from the computer and pacing around like he always did when he was deep in thought. "I'm going to go ask my mom right away about that shock-mounted condenser microphone. We really shouldn't waste any time."

I didn't know what he was talking about. Time was one thing we had. It was a lazy Monday and there were weeks of summer vacation ahead of us. Every day we biked over to Other Mike's house, being centrally located and all. Mike and I watched baseball, Other Mike read books about warlocks. We played video games. We put in some appearances at the library, and I read a lot of the baseball books. I even read one or two about history, but let's be honest: I wasn't exactly on pace for two hundred. How did someone actually read two hundred books in a summer? I shuddered to think. They probably went blind from eyestrain and possibly insane from boredom. They probably lived in an asylum now.

"The deadline isn't for three weeks," Mike said. "It'd probably take you about three minutes to whip up a video."

"Well, thank you for recognizing my obvious skills," Other Mike said, breathing on his glasses and cleaning them on his shirt.

"You go rush off to Best Buy with Mommy," Mike said. "Leonard and I are going to be on the lawn couch. Businessperson's special today. Early game time: twelve-oh-five."

"But—but—but it's Best Buy!" Other Mike said. He didn't seem to understand that baseball games were not to be missed. And he really liked Best Buy.

"Dude, we have snacks," Mike sang. "Best Buy cannot compete with the lawn couch and snacks."

Other Mike agreed, reluctantly, and we cruised over to Mike's lawn couch. It was plastic and had an "old shoe" smell due to being sort of damp all the time, but it was great. We flipped on the TV (using the waterproof remote control Mike's dad made out of a regular remote and a sandwich baggie) and opened up some cheese balls. The TV was under an overhang, shielded from the rain and in perfect view of the couch. The first thing we saw when the tube flickered to life? The commercial for the Armchair Announcer contest. "You could be in the booth!" Buck Foltz's ridiculous hair called to me like a sign from above.

The Phils game was a good one. Famosa made a couple of throwing errors but got a big double and they won, 6–5. Day games are cool, but we weren't quite sure what to do with the evening, but then Mike's dad came out back. As always, he had a bag of snacks in his hand and a big smile on his round face. Also, this time, he had something else: a book.

"Gentlemen," he said. "I had to stop in at the library on the way home, so I picked this up off the new-book shelf. Looked like something you might enjoy."

He was right! *Wacky Baseball Lists* was the title—just the kind of book Mike and I loved. The first thing I noticed about the cover was that it included a picture of 1970s Yankees star Oscar Gamble—owner of probably the greatest hair in baseball history. The cover included a collage of other baseball personalities too. We knew most of them—Barry Bonds, Cal Ripken Jr., Joe Mauer— but there was one guy we didn't recognize.

"Hey, who's that?" I asked. It was an ancient picture in the corner of the cover, a grainy image of a grumpy old-time lefty making a toss off a small mound.

None of us had a clue.

I found a page with a code explaining who everyone on the cover was. The grump in question was a guy named "Blaze" O'Farrell, who turned out to be a pitcher for the 1944 Philadelphia Blue Jays.

"The Blue Jays?" I said.

"That's right," Mike's dad said. "The Phils were called the Blue Jays in the 1940s, for some reason."

"Weird!" I said.

"Still stunk, though," Mike's dad said.

Blaze sure did. The list he was on was "worst ERAs in history." To figure out a pitcher's ERA, or earned run average, you divide the number of runs he gave up by the number of innings pitched. It's a major tool for measuring how good a pitcher is. O'Farrell, it turned out, was not very good.

A one-page chapter explained that O'Farrell

played in just one game. It was June 15, 1944. He made the team after a bunch of starting pitchers got sent to fight in World War II. After that one game, he himself got sent to war. He survived the war, the book said, but never pitched again. His whole career was that one bad game. That one *very* bad game. He got just one out after giving up seven earned runs in the top of the first. There were other guys on the list who had given up a run without ever getting an out, giving them an ERA of infinity, but no one in all of recorded baseball history had ever given up more runs on fewer outs than Blaze. Most guys have an ERA around 4. Blaze's earned run average was a staggering 189— the worst of all time.

"Why did they call him 'Blaze'?" Other Mike wanted to know.

"Couldn't have been because of his fastball," I said, thinking about his terrible record.

"I wonder if he's still alive?" Mike asked, and then quickly added, "Nah, he must be dead."

"If he played ball in '44, he's probably only about eighty-nine," Other Mike said. Other Mike liked to do calculations in his head. He didn't even use his fingers, just pointed his blue eyes up to the sky, like the answers were written up there. He thought it impressed people, but, shockingly, it really didn't ever seem to.

"Oh, *only* eighty-nine?" Mike scoffed. "Yeah, he's probably still playing ball. He's probably still in the minors, waiting for his callback to the big leagues."

"We should write him a letter," I said. "I bet he doesn't get a lot of fan mail."

"Especially not if he's dead," Mike said.

"I'm sure he's alive," Other Mike said, rubbing his hands together. "You know how they say only the good die young? Blaze O'Farrell will probably live to one hundred!"

At this, we all cracked up. Other Mike's laugh is like a cross between a car horn and a lawn mower. Mike's dad was laughing too. Even Mike's little sister, Arianna, was laughing, although she probably didn't get the joke. I didn't even notice her come out and flop on the lawn couch. That's how excited I was about the book and the tale of Blaze O'Farrell.

"So, Lenny," Mike's dad said. "You gonna go for Armchair Announcer? When I saw that commercial, I thought of you right away."

"I might do it," I said. "But I don't know what

I'd talk about in the video— Of course!" My voice cracked as I yelled this last part. Arianna laughed at me, but I didn't care. Mike's dad had just given me a gift even greater than cheese balls. Now I had the perfect moment to re-create for the contest: Blaze O'Farrell's short trip to the majors.

"Hey, Other Mike," I said, breaking the silence. "Can you make a video look like it's sixty years old on your computer?"

"Sure," Other Mike said. "I can generate some auto-grain and add random dust particles and drop the color out to sepia tones—"

"I have no idea what you're talking about," I said, cutting him off. "But I think I'm onto something."

"What?" the Mikes asked in unison.

"Meet first thing tomorrow morning at Other Mike's and we'll totally win that contest," I said.

"Totally," Mike said.

"Totally," Other Mike said.

"Totally."

I headed back home in time for Norbeck family dinner. Or at least that was the idea. Courtney was gone, which was nice. Mom and Dad were there, eating, technically, but mostly running around the house shoving pizza in their mouths. Work was theoretically over for the day, but Dad had a meeting at the hospital that evening and Mom made it clear that she had exciting plans to retreat to her home office and read about ventricles or whatever she did in there. I grabbed a slice or two for myself and went up to my room, where I usually eat my meals. At least the pizza was good. Pepperoni from Angelo's.

I picked off the pieces one by one, announcing the act out loud. It was stupid, but it made me laugh. *And Lenny Norbeck puts ANOTHER piece of pepperoni into his mouth. The crowd goes wild! Ahhhh-ahhhh-ahhh!* I can make a really good crowd noise by breathing through my hands in a certain way. It sounds great. Of course at that moment Dad looked in and shook his bald head at me. Clearly I had disappointed him again.

"Can't you do something productive with your time for once, Lenny?" he said. "Life is not a baseball game."

Shut up, Dad, I thought. *I'm going to win this contest. Everyone is going to be in awe of my amazing announcing skills. You'll ask me for my autograph and I won't even give you one.* Maybe life *is* a baseball game. And maybe I'm about to win it.

CHAPTER THREE

"This—this—this insufferable turd!" Mike stammered.

As planned, we met first thing the next morning (or, you know, noon) at Other Mike's house. Courtney kept trying to make me clean my room, so I had to get out of there. My room wasn't even that messy. Sure, there were a few piles of clothes on the floor and books heaped everywhere, but I was *supposed* to be reading a lot, right? Other Mike's room, however, was always very tidy. The clothes were on hangers and his bookshelves were well organized, filled with neatly stacked books and small statues of wizards. Maybe warlocks. I could never tell them apart.

I had intended to present my plan for Armchair Announcer, but Mike was hunched over Other Mike's computer and fuming at the screen. He had recently discovered BedrosiansBeard.com—a little corner of the Internet filled with crazy Phils fans. The name came from an old Phil, Steve Bedrosian. Steve Bedrosian was a pretty good pitcher for a few years a while ago and did have a nice beard, but I'm not quite sure it deserved its own website. But that's the Internet for you, I guess. And, yes, you'd better believe that I know it's a little ironic for me to call anyone a "crazy Phils fan." We're crazy, yeah, and we're big-time fans, but some of these dudes were seriously nuts.

"This jerkwad calls himself PhilzFan1 but spends all his time ripping 'em!" Mike said. "How can he possibly be the number one fan if he basically hates the team?"

"Don't let it bother you," Other Mike said. "Putting a *1* after your screen name doesn't actually make you legally the number one fan. Sheesh."

"But—but—but," Mike stammered.

Other Mike laughed. "You said 'butt,'" he said.

"Shut up! This isn't funny! PhilzFan1 said that R. J. Weathers is on steroids and still is going to end up sucking," Mike said.

R. J. Weathers was a top Phillies prospect. He was only nineteen, but there was a lot of talk about him being the next great pitching star. He was tearing up the minor leagues with a ninety-five-mile-an-hour fastball and a unique pitch of his own invention that supposedly fluttered like a butterfly in a windstorm.

We were completely in awe of RJ, even Other Mike, who didn't really care about baseball that much. I definitely didn't like PhilzFan1 saying that RJ was on steroids, but I also didn't like seeing Mike get so worked up. He can get grumpy quickly, and I didn't feel like dealing with Angry Mike.

"Weathers hasn't even pitched a game for us yet," I said. "Relax."

"Then PhilzFan1 called Famosa a woman," Mike said. "He said they should make him a special uniform with a dress."

"Well, even I find that offensive," Other Mike said, frowning. "He's clearly not a woman. Isn't he the Mexican guy with the silly mustache?"

"Why do we even hang out with him?" Mike asked me, pointing a stubby finger toward Other Mike. "Famosa is *Dominican* and his mustache rules."

"You hang out with me because there's more to life than baseball?" Other Mike responded, hoisting a warlock statue hopefully.

Mike gave him the most skeptical face in the

world. Like you had just told him that sleep wasn't important or that nachos were not the greatest food ever.

"Dudes," I said, shaking my head. "It is time to focus on our entry. We will win this contest, and whatever some schmuck on the Internet says will be way too insignificant to care about."

"I guess you're right," Mike said. But while he said it, he kept typing. I noticed his finger going a lot to Shift and then 1, which meant he was getting carried away with exclamation points again.

"You're flaming him right now, aren't you?" I asked.

"Why ever would you say that?" he asked, not even trying to hide the clatter of the keys.

I looked at the screen. It said: "PHILZFAN1, YOU ARE A NUMBER TWO!!!!!!!!!!!!!!!!!!!!!!"

I reached over and pressed the Off button to put the computer out of its misery.

"Take a deep breath," said Other Mike. "Walk it off."

"Let's focus on the video," I said. I told them my plan: "We go old-school for the Armchair Announcer. You know plenty of people are going to do re-creations of the World Series wins or something, but I want to do a moment no one else is thinking about. I want to do Blaze O'Farrell. . . . Although I'm not quite sure how on earth we could film something that would look like 1944. . . ."

"Captain Magnificent Superterrific to the rescue!" Other Mike said, jumping into the air. (Captain Magnificent Superterrific was one of his attempts at giving himself a new nickname to replace Other Mike. Shockingly, it did not stick. He was the only one who used it.) His glasses slid off his face, and he scrambled to put them back on, talking quickly. "I just had a great idea! My new camera has the seven-point-one upgrade, which includes roto capability and comes bundled with a free green screen!" He started digging through his closet.

"English, please," I said. I again had no idea what he was talking about.

"It means," Other Mike explained, readjusting his shorts, "that we can film you against this green sheet and then make the backdrop whatever we want." He held up the green sheet and waved it like a bullfighter's cape.

"That green sheet can make it look like I'm at the ballpark?"

"Exactly," he said. "It can make it look like you're *anywhere*."

"Great," Mike said. But he was distracted. Somehow he had turned the computer back on and thus had resumed yelling about PhilzFan1.

"You really need to let it go," Other Mike said.

"I will *not* let it go!" Mike said. "Check out this one!" He read the next post from PhilzFan1: "This team is a disgrace. If you're a real fan, you'd stop rooting for these losers to win again and would spend your energy hoping for something that actually has a chance of happening. Like pigs flying. Or a snowball fight in Hawaii. I was thinking about calling for a boycott of this pathetic excuse for a baseball team, but what good would a boycott do? We need more drastic action. Check back here for further instructions. . . ."

"What on earth could that mean?" I asked.

"'Drastic action'?" Other Mike said.

"'Further instructions'?" I said. "Okay, that part makes sense. But 'drastic action'? It's almost like PhilzFan1 is actually making a threat."

The Phils were having a rough year and hardly winning as many games as we would have liked. But why was this guy so angry? I wondered if he was a gambler and had a lot of money riding on the

Phillies' success. Since they were losing, would he take "drastic action" to make sure they won? And what did he mean by that—blackmail? Or maybe even . . . murder?

"Focus!" Other Mike said. "Let me in there." He elbowed Mike away from the computer, and his fingers started flying. He always typed incredibly fast, and sometimes he even hit the right keys. Before long he had what he wanted. He found a great picture of Shibe Park—the old stadium where Blaze had his massive blaze of stinking. "Background done," he said. "Now we just have to film you here. And then I can work my magic. It will look exactly like you're at Shibe."

"Yeah," I said. "Now all I have to do is figure out what to say."

"Lenny Norbeck, the boy with the golden voice," they both said at once. Then they looked at me and smiled, their Mike faces stretched and beaming with what seemed like pride.

Did they really have that much confidence in me? Or were they making fun of me? I didn't feel that sure of myself. I could do a good announcer voice, yeah. And it was easy playing announcer on the lawn couch with the Mikes as my only audience. But this would be seen by judges! It could be my big break! I started to panic. I felt my heart climb up my throat. I didn't think I'd be able to get *any* words out! I'd just babble and blather like a lunatic! Everyone would laugh at me.

"How much time do I have to figure it out?" I asked. My voice squeaked at the end. I hated when it did that.

The Mikes laughed.

"It's fine if you're nervous," Mike said, ignoring my question and patting me on the shoulder. "I still get nervous when I have to floss my teeth."

Other Mike and I looked at each other for a long moment. At the same second, we both cracked up.

"Who gets nervous about flossing?" Other Mike said, sputtering, laughing so hard he could barely get the words out. I almost felt bad. *Almost.*

"Shut up," Mike said. "Sometimes it makes you bleed. Never mind. Whatever. Let's get to work."

"We have time, Flossie," Other Mike said. "We still have to find out some more stuff about Blaze and what exactly went down at that game so Lenny has something to announce about."

I breathed a sigh of relief. They weren't making fun of me. The Mikes were going to help me. Of course they were—they were my best friends. And with their help, maybe I'd actually win this thing.

CHAPTER FOUR

The next day, I made Mom happy by telling her I had big plans to spend the whole day at the library. It was true, but not because I was trying to shatter that reading club record. I had research to do. Armchair Announcer research. I figured that we could get a little more information on Blaze's story and then I'd know what to say.

The Mikes rode with me, all three of us wearing our matching red helmets. Sometimes we liked to pretend we were a motorcycle gang. "You ready, Killer?" Other Mike said. "You ready, Snake Eyes?" He gave us different biker nicknames every time we rode anywhere. It always made me laugh.

Mike got to the library first because he liked to show off his strength by sprinting his bike the last one hundred yards or so. Schwenkfelder Public Library was not a huge building; basically, it was a tall wooden rectangle that maybe used to be a barn. It always made me happy when we went there, as long as I didn't have homework to do. As usual, I came in second and Other Mike huffed up in third place.

The librarian, Mr. Bonzer, had a big smile and a bushy beard. He was a cool guy. He was a baseball fan too. Every once in a while he wore a wide red and blue tie with a noticeable Phillies *P* on the bottom, and he had a big blowup of the "PHILLIES WIN" newspaper headline tacked to his desk after they won the World Series.

"Hello, sir," I said.

"Boys. Can I help you?" he said. His bald head glistened as he smiled. He dabbed at his sweaty forehead with a handkerchief.

"Yeah," Mike said. "Maybe you *can* help us!" Bonzer nodded politely, wiggling his large fingers like an evil genius. Mike continued: "We want to find out some information on an old ballplayer. His name was 'Blaze' O'Farrell. There's a little thing about him in that new book my dad got from here."

"*Wacky Baseball Lists,*" Bonzer said.

Impressive. Did he have all the books memorized?

"So here's the thing. That book has, like, a

single page—O'Farrell had the worst ERA in history. He pitched one-third of an inning in 1944 and then got shipped off to war."

"Tough break," Bonzer said, saluting. "What more do you want to know?"

"We want to know exactly what happened in that game. How did he give up all those runs? The book doesn't say."

"We also want to know if he's still alive," Other Mike chimed in. "Write him a letter or something, if he is. I think he's totally alive. Also, we sort of need to know if you have that new book in the warlock series. . . ."

It sounded crazy the way we were explaining it. We didn't even mention the contest. We just seemed nuts. Like the kind of guys who spent all day threatening people on the Internet. But Bonzer seemed to have a high capacity for weird. He fielded our request seriously.

"*Warlock Wallop Five* is already on reserve for you, Other Mike," he said. "It will be here in a few days. And finding out what happened in that game should be pretty easy if you have the exact date."

"June 15, 1944." We all said it at once in perfect unison, like a three-headed boy.

"Sure, yeah," Bonzer said. "You know it's scary

how you three share a brain, right?" He pushed his large frame off the chair and got to his feet. "We have every Philly paper going back a hundred years on microfilm. We can just look up the sports section. There had to be a write-up."

He escorted us into the microfilm room. It was all dark in there, and they had these little film-projector-looking things. The room smelled historical and the machines made cool noises. They whirred and clicked like the beginning of a movie. Big old cabinets held tiny scans of every newspaper for the past century.

"The paper from the sixteenth will probably have the story on your game," Bonzer said. He popped the film in and flicked a knob. The machine whirred, and a grainy image of a 1944 baseball game popped to life.

"There you go, gentlemen," he said. "It's a quarter if you want a print."

We jostled for position in front of the screen. Mike was the strongest so he got the best seat. He puffed out his wide shoulders, nearly knocking us over.

"BLUE JAYS FALL TO CUBS," he read, scanning the headline. "So weird seeing the Phils called the Blue Jays."

"Yeah," I said. "Didn't make them play any better, either." The final score was 10–1.

"Hey, look at this," Mike said. "Blaze's real name was Blair."

"Blair is my aunt's name! Sorta explains the nickname," Other Mike blurted out.

Mike kept reading. "Hey, and the only out he got was by using the hidden-ball trick!"

The hidden-ball trick, if you didn't know, is just what it sounds like. The pitcher pretends to have the ball while a fielder hides it in his glove. When the runner takes his lead, the fielder tags him out. It's actually really hard because the pitcher can't be on the mound without the ball or he'll get called for a balk and the runner gets to advance a base for free. So he has to act all casual while pretending he has the ball. It's tough to pull this off. Old Blaze obviously wasn't much of a pitcher, but he must have been a pretty good actor.

"Here's the box score," Mike said, pressing the button on the microfilm thing. "That'll give us the details. Wow, look at this! 'Putsy' Caballero played for the '44 team."

We all laughed. Putsy Caballero. Funniest baseball name ever? (Okay, maybe not, because the following were all actual players, I swear: Estel

Crabtree, Van Lingle Mungo, Harry Colliflower, and Tony Suck. Really.) "We can't know exactly what went down," Mike said. "The article doesn't say much. But we can make a pretty good guess. Looks like he didn't give up that many hits. Mostly walks, I suppose."

"That's not going to be much fun to re-create," I said, scratching my chin. "Ball four, ball four, ball four."

"You can make it fun," Other Mike said, punching my arm. "I know you can do it. It'll be great."

Mike read more from the screen. He was trying to whisper, but "library voices" have never been our strong suit. "Looks like there was one home run—Bill Nicholson went yard for Chicago."

"Nicholson goes yard," I said in an old-fashioned announcer's voice. The Mikes laughed.

Bonzer came back into the room. He shushed us halfheartedly, but I had a feeling he was getting excited too. Besides, the room was empty. "Do you have what you need, guys?"

"Yeah!" we said together at the exact same moment. Bonzer smiled and shook his head. "Let's print it out!" we said in unison. Bonzer laughed.

"I have some more stuff for you," he said. He

was holding a printout of his own. "Did you know that O'Farrell's first name was Blair?"

"Yeah," I said. "Explains why he went by a nickname."

"Well, I found that in an online baseball encyclopedia, and then I put Blair O'Farrell into a white pages directory."

"And?"

"He's alive."

"Whoa!"

"And he lives in Schwenkfelder."

What else was there to say to that except "Double whoa!"

"Here's his address," Bonzer said. "Librarian's honor."

The Mikes and I looked at each other. Then we looked at Bonzer. Then we looked at each other. Could we go visit Blair—I mean, Blaze—at his house?

We thanked Mr. Bonzer and headed out. We put our helmets on. "Pretty productive trip, wouldn't you say, Sharkface?" Mike said.

"Sharkface?" I laughed.

"Hey, it's hard coming up with different biker names every time we ride anywhere. You try it." Then he sped ahead, leaving us in the dust. By the time we made it back to Other Mike's house, Mike had already let himself in.

"So we have Blaze's address, gentlemen," Mike said once Other Mike and I had joined him in Other Mike's bedroom. "What are we going to do with it?" He was standing in the middle of the room, pacing slightly.

"Beats me," I said, flopping onto the floor.

"Hold on," Other Mike puffed. He was all sweaty and still breathing hard from the bike ride but already at his computer. He was typing quickly and clicking all over the screen, like the computer was part of him. "Ta-da!" he said. "We follow this map." Blaze did seem to live within biking distance, according to the map. Other Mike was amazingly fast with the computer.

"We're not really going over there, right?" I said from my spot on the floor.

"Why not?" Other Mike said, standing over me. "Are you afraid of him?"

"I'm not afraid," I said, sitting up. "But he *was* in the war."

"He's, like, a hundred years old! And besides, they don't let you bring home guns from war. Wait, do they? Did they even *have* guns in World War II?"

"Yes, they had guns in World War II," I said. "They had tanks too." I knew a lot about World War II, mainly because of a book I read from the library about the baseball player Moe Berg. Once, Moe supposedly hid a camera in his kimono on a trip to Japan to sneak pictures of the Japanese army. He also was involved in a plot to assassinate Nazis who were trying to get the atomic bomb. Plus, he was a catcher who got his first start because Phillies catcher Frank Bruggy was so fat that the pitcher refused to pitch to him. See, Mom? I'm totally enriching myself.

"Do you think Blaze has his own tank?" Other Mike said. He started pretending like he was steering a tank. It was sort of childish, but I laughed.

"I'm sure he has a tank," Mike said. "Yeah." He rolled his eyes.

"All right, gentlemen," I said, doing my best to look serious. "I have an idea." Thinking about Moe Berg made me feel like I should be at least a little brave. Plus, remembering that story about his secret mission gave me an idea. No, not kimonos. But, yes: disguises.

"All right, Michaels," I said. I jumped up from the floor and started pacing. "We can dress like Cub Scouts and go to Blaze's house."

"Wait, why do we have to dress like Cub Scouts?" Mike said, folding his arms over his chest.

"Why else would we knock on his door?" I asked.

"I don't get it," Other Mike said. "Girl Scouts are the ones always knocking on people's doors. Selling cookies. And aren't we a little old for Cub Scouts?"

"Stevie Fart-Sniffer is still in Scouts," I said. "And Cub Scouts could go door-to-door. Remember that time we did the food drive? We had to go around collecting canned food for poor people."

"Not bad," Mike said, looking intrigued. He brushed back his hair with one hand. "All we have to do is get to his house dressed as Cub Scouts. We bring a bag or something to say it's for canned goods. He gives us some beans or whatever, we ask him his name, he tells us."

"I see where you're going with this," Other Mike said. He started drumming his fingers on his desk excitedly. "Then we act like, 'Hey, Blair O'Farrell . . . why does that name sound familiar?'"

I smiled. They were getting it. "Yeah," I said. "We pretend we know his name—a former major league player and war hero we read about in school!" I felt pretty good and gave the guys a wide smile and a salute. "Then we tell him that we're big Phillies fans, and we try to get him to talk a little bit about his time in the majors. Maybe we get a few facts about him that weren't in the papers."

Mike was smiling too. He was totally on board. "Maybe we even get him to let us take his picture!" he said. "Maybe he could be in the video! We'll be the first people to interview Blaze O'Farrell in fifty years. It'll make the video a winner. More YouTube hits than that cat who can walk on two legs."

"Technically, the fine announcing skills of the boy with the golden voice will make it a winner," I said, trying to convince myself this was actually true. "Ahem. But, yeah, that's the idea. Now, there is the small matter of the disguises. . . ."

The three of us were Cub Scouts together for years, so our closets were filled with all manner of Scouting clothing. We agreed to dig out something suitable and meet back at Other Mike's house. I pedaled home as fast as I could and went searching for some old Scouting stuff.

I found the box after a short dig through the mound of junk in my closet. The hat was okay. I just had to adjust the strap a bit. It was weird to think about how much your head grows. You never notice your head getting bigger. But man, it sure does. Courtney came into my room. "Nice look," she said.

"Yeah," I grunted.

"What are you up to?"

"Um, we're thinking about getting back into Scouts," I lied. "You know, like Stevie Fart-Sniffer. Um, I gotta go." She rolled her eyes and popped her gum, which was her response to everything. I didn't care. "Go tan yourself," I muttered, hoping she didn't hear me.

I hopped back on my bike and headed for Other Mike's. I got there quickly, pulling at my stupid tiny shirt to try to stretch it out. Other Mike and Mike were waiting for me on the front lawn. Other Mike was wearing his Scout neckerchief over his mouth.

"What is that look?" I said. "We're not robbing a bank here."

"I thought you said we needed disguises," he said.

I rolled my eyes, Courtney-style, and looked over at Mike. His clothes fit even worse than mine. (Unlike Other Mike, who has apparently been the same size ever since we quit Scouts.) I didn't want to say anything. It was really nice of him to look so ridiculous and uncomfortable. Let's face it—this was *my* plan and *my* contest. I was the one who had this absurd disguises idea. "Let's get going, troops," I said.

"Follow me!" Other Mike said.

"But you're always the slowest," Mike complained.

"Yeah, but I got the directions," he said. "This time you can't ride ahead." He waved the printout with the map in the air like a victory flag. He almost steered into a shrub. "It's hard to read and steer!" he yelled. Then he added, "Someday I'm going to invent a GPS for bikes. I'll be rich." It did sound like a pretty good idea.

After a little while we ended up in a neighborhood I had never seen before. It wasn't very far from us—just a few miles, but in an out-of-the-way area. The houses were smaller, older. Some of them looked like trailers or train cars. Following the map and searching for addresses on the rusty mailboxes led us to Blaze's house. It was a scary-looking place. The windows were covered with dark curtains, the lawn was dead, and an ancient rusty car sat on blocks in the driveway.

"I wouldn't be surprised if he *did* have a tank out back," Other Mike said. It was that kind of house. The kind of house where you honestly would not have been surprised to find a World War II tank out back. I didn't want to find out. The yard looked like it was filled with poison and burrs. Maybe snakes. Possibly traps that would clamp onto your leg and you'd have to chew off your foot like a bear. We took a deep breath, argued about who should be the one to ring the doorbell, and then forced Other Mike to do it.

"Who cares?" he said. "It's just pushing the doorbell." But he was scared. We all were a little scared, even though no one would admit it. "Hey, there *is* no doorbell," he said. "And I'm not knocking." He backed away.

"Why is knocking scarier than ringing the doorbell?" I said. No one moved. I realized it was up to me. I marched right up to the door and knocked on it. There was no answer. I pretended to be disappointed, but I was actually happy. The whole scene was starting to creep me out, and the whole idea of Blaze or Blair or whatever was a bit terrifying.

"Let's get out of here," Other Mike said. "I feel like someone is watching us."

I felt it too. Or at least I thought I did. But I wasn't giving up. I pounded on the door a few times as hard as I could with my knuckles. The door was old and the wood was soft. My hand left a dent. Oops. We waited a few seconds. There was still no answer. I felt happy that I had knocked like a man, though, and if nothing happened, nothing happened.

I turned to face the Mikes and shrug, but when I looked, they were gone. A second later I heard a whisper. "Lenny! Over here!"

I looked and saw them on the side of the house, kicking at an old rusty bin. "What are you guys doing?"

"He's obviously not home," Other Mike said. "Thought I'd see what this thing was."

"It's a garbage can, genius," I said. "Old-timers burn their garbage."

"Isn't that against the law?" Other Mike asked.

"What are you, the garbage police?" Mike asked him.

"Your mom is the garbage police," Other Mike said. To punctuate this brilliant insult, he reached in and grabbed something from the bin and threw it at Mike.

"Ah!" Mike yelled. "Ew! I can't believe you threw garbage! What is it?"

"It's, like, a pill bottle," Other Mike said. "It won't kill you, you big baby."

Mike picked up the bottle.

"N-n-nitroglycerin," he stammered.

I shrieked. Then I yelled, "Nitroglycerin is an explosive!" One of the history books I read was about spies. In it this spy tricked the Nazis by using a vial of nitroglycerin! "Back away from that, Michael!" I said. "Back away slowly."

He took my advice, sort of. He didn't back away slowly. He ran away from the bottle, toward his bike. He already had one foot on a pedal when we heard the front door open. It groaned, like it hadn't been opened in a long time.

Mike was already gone. Other Mike and I were scrambling to get back toward our bikes, trying to go fast, but not *too* fast, through the thicket of Blaze O'Farrell's yard. If he had nitroglycerin in that barrel, what else might he have?

We moved quickly and carefully. And then we noticed Blaze in the doorway. He had a bottle in each hand. He was very old—gray hair and a gray face. He was also raising his leg, slowly rocking into what looked like a pitching windup.

"Um, is he going to throw those bottles at us?" Other Mike asked me.

"I think he is! Run!"

We didn't worry about booby traps anymore,

we just wanted to move. A bottle zipped by, a few inches from my head! We really started to run then, scrambling for our bikes. Blaze wasn't a good pitcher, and he was about one hundred years old, but he was really chucking those bottles! We scurried back to the street, where we had stashed our bikes, but Blaze kept throwing bottles at us. One soared over our heads and smashed on the street, where it exploded like a little grenade with a fantastic shattering noise.

Other Mike and I hopped onto our bikes, bottles still flying at us like bombs dropping from an airplane. The old man had a heck of an arm! I was worried about Other Mike getting caught behind and nailed by a bottle, but I figured I wouldn't do anyone a favor by getting myself brained. Fear made me pedal hard, harder than I ever had before, so hard I thought the chain on my bike might pop or my legs might rip out of their sockets. Other Mike must have been feeling it too because I had never seen him ride so fast.

I looked back and saw Other Mike's face just a few yards behind me. It was as bright red as a Phillies hat. He also looked like he was holding back a smile. We were almost all the way back to Other Mike's house before I could think it was even a little funny.

CHAPTER FIVE

We met back at Other Mike's house the next day. I waved to his mom on the way in. She was out in the yard planting some flowers. Other Mike probably trampled the old ones. Again. "Staying out of trouble, Lenny?" she asked, wiping some dirt off her nose with her pink gardening glove.

"Sure thing, Mrs. Other Mike," I said. "Hey, is my mom paying you to ask that?" She laughed. I wasn't trying to be funny. Mrs. Other Mike was always laughing. She was as plump and short as Mr. Other Mike was tall and skinny. Standing next to each other, they looked like the number ten. Other Mike definitely took after his dad— with his short-cropped hair and lanky limbs, he hardly looked anything like the smiling Mrs. Other Mike.

"He's up in his room with Mike," she said,

pointing to the upper level of the house. "Probably on the computer."

"Probably," I said, ditching my bike on the lawn.

Other Mike actually wasn't at the computer when I got up there. He was pacing around like a caged panther, fidgeting with his glasses, wildly excited about his ideas for the video.

"All right," he said, exhaling loudly. "Forget Blaze, he's crazy. We don't need him."

"Do you think I still have a chance to win?" I asked.

"Of course," Other Mike said, waving his arm in the air. "I cannot imagine that most of these baseball fans have a computer genius at their disposal. It's simple—I'll start with a close shot of this headline and then Ken-Burns it out to you, Leonard, in front of the green screen." He was talking very fast. I just nodded.

I had spent the night researching, writing, thinking about, and practicing my part. The challenge was just to create a *moment* in Phillies' baseball history, but this was a peculiar moment—it wouldn't be easy. I'd looked up a website about lingo from the 1940s and got all sorts of funny expressions to use. I'd also grabbed my one nice suit and borrowed an old hat of my dad's. For some reason, it really seemed like I should have a mustache, so I drew one on with a marker. I just hoped it would come off.

We hung the green screen in the corner of Other Mike's room. I stood in front, and Other Mike said, "Action." I took a deep breath, and it all came rolling out:

"Hello, folks out there in radio land," I said. "Leonard Norbeck here bringing you the afternoon action between the Cubbies of Chi-Town and your Philly Blue Jays. It's a warm day here at Shibe Park, and a new hurler for the hometown nine is taking the hill. They call him Blaze, and hi-de-ho, let's hope his heater lives up to his name."

The Mikes laughed silently in the corner. I was off to a good start. "It's the top of the first, and Blaze is having a little trouble with his command here," I continued. "He's as wild as an alley cat in a street fight. Three men on already and Cubbie slugger Bill Nicholson's up to the plate. He's gammin' about, strutting his stuff. Here's the windup, the pitch, and, oh, sweet mercy—Nicholson hits one deep over the right-field bleachers. Good night, Irene. Kiss it good-bye. Cubs up, four to zilch."

The Mikes were fighting hard not to crack up. It was going great!

"And now Dewey Williams steps into the box. And he laces the first pitch to right field for a single. Oh my. The throw comes in and first baseman Tony Lupien walks it over to O'Farrell. They're chatting at the mound. Next batter is Stan Hack. Williams takes his lead off of first and— What's this? The umpire calls the runner out! It's the old hidden-ball trick! I'll be snookered! Isn't that the cat's pajamas? O'Farrell and Lupien pull off some razzle-dazzle here in this jalopy of a first. Ain't that swell?" I said, almost cracking myself up.

"Now, just one down and another run comes in, and, yep, here comes the skipper with the hook. That's finally it for Blaze. Seven runs against just one out. Not the finest debut for the young hurler. The boys have some work to do if they want to come back in this one. . . ."

And just like that, it was done. One take. It was so strange—sort of a blur, really. I'd spent all this time thinking about it, but actually doing it happened without a thought. *Was* being an announcer really "my thing"? It sure felt pretty awesome, and this was just me and the Mikes talking about a game from fifty years ago. How great would it be to actually be there in the booth at a real game, talking to millions as it happened? I didn't say any of this to the Mikes. I just said, "Um, was that okay?"

Mike and Other Mike stared at me in amazement. "It was incredible!" they said at once.

"I'm not exactly sure what you were talking about," Other Mike said. "But it sounded wonderful."

Mike rolled his eyes. "How did you do that?" Mike asked.

"I don't know," I said. "I practiced a little last night, and . . . it just came out."

"I knew you were good, Lenny," Other Mike said. "But I didn't know you were *that* good."

"Um, thanks?" I said.

"It's going to look even better when I spiff it up." Other Mike hooked up the camera to his computer and got to work adding fade-outs and wacky jazz music and credits. Mike and Other Mike argued about who would get listed as what in the credits, but I didn't listen. My work was done. I sat back and relaxed. We uploaded the video to the Phillies website, and that was that. Doing the upload was so easy. Just a click of the mouse. Just moving a finger a tiny bit. And to think how much it changed everything. . . .

* * *

Two weeks later and six innings into a Phillies losing effort, my cell phone rang. I was over on the lawn couch, like I'd been most days, just watching the game and hanging with the Mikes. Mom had more or less dropped the idea of me taking enrichment classes, and I was keeping up my end of the bargain. Okay, I wasn't quite breaking the record for most books read over the summer, but I was scraping by. Mr. Bonzer even told Mom as much; thankfully, he didn't mention that basically every book I read was about baseball.

The call was my mom. What she had to say was this: "Leonard—weird thing. We just got a call. Man said he was from the Phillies. Said you won some contest? Armoire Announcer, I think. Do you know anything about this? He said you're supposed to be at the ballpark on July twenty-ninth, but I'm already scheduled to work late and . . ."

I tried to answer, but words were not coming out clearly. The Phillies called me? I won the contest? *I won the contest!* "July twenty-ninth?! I'll, um, explain later, Mom," I said. I hung up.

I won the contest? I won the contest! The Mikes were crowding me on the lawn couch, pumping their fists.

"Was that . . . ?"

"Is it . . . ?"

I smiled and nodded, and they mobbed me. It felt like I just hit the game-winning home run and the whole team was high-fiving me at once. We celebrated nonstop. We put the date on the calendar: July 29. Three weeks away. I circled it with a thick marker. I wouldn't stop smiling until then.

Even Mom and Dad seemed a little excited about it, and forgot about bugging me to do something "productive" with my time. Courtney was still around all the time, but I was getting pretty good at ignoring her.

Dad and I made plans: he would come to the park with me. I was allowed one guest in the booth, and he said he wouldn't miss it. I was sort of shocked, actually. I expected he wouldn't want to come, or wouldn't care at all. I'd get to announce a game with all of my favorite players on the field—and maybe R. J. Weathers! Get this: rumor had it he was going to come up from the minors and pitch his first game in late July. I wondered if I'd get to meet him. Little did I know I would watch him die.

CHAPTER SIX

Before I knew it, July twenty-ninth had arrived. Okay, it wasn't *before* I knew it. I realized it was coming. I was very aware of the fact that the date was coming. It was circled on the calendar and I stared at it every day, counting the days. Sometimes I'd do the calculations and try to figure out the number of hours, but that felt a bit too much like math homework.

The game I'd be announcing was an evening one, but I was still up early that day. Actually, I don't think I slept at all. The night was a blur of nerves and trips to the bathroom. I was so excited and jittery about doing my inning that it was like *I* was R. J. Weathers. And, yup, the young pitcher was set to pitch his first game that very night. I was thrilled, yet terrified. Like I was actually going to be pitching against the Mets and not just announcing. I spent the whole day pacing around and praying that I wouldn't embarrass myself. What if my voice cracked during my inning? What if I said something totally stupid and millions of people heard it? What if I didn't say anything at all and just filled the booth with awkward silence? I spent an hour choosing which Phillies shirt to wear. Finally, it was time to head to the game with Dad.

Every time I walked into the ballpark, it took my breath away a little. I spent so much time watching games on TV that I almost forgot it was a real place. Being there in the flesh was strange. It felt like I was stepping into a cartoon or a mythical place that existed only in a book. Like if you could just go hang out with Harry Potter in person or eat a hot dog with Luke Skywalker or get a pet Pokémon.

The trip was all the more magical this time because I walked in through the VIP entrance. Dad explained that it meant *very* important person. I was never even an important person, much less a *very* important person. It felt pretty great. We were early, but there was already a crowd gathering. A murmur of excitement was everywhere. ESPN camera crews were there to cover the event—R. J.

Weathers making his debut was big news. Phillies fans were out in force. A sea of red shirts filled the stands and the smell of cheesesteaks scented the air. I flashed the VIP badge they had sent us in the mail, and a security guard took me and Dad up a back elevator and through hallways usually reserved for players and staff.

As we got off the elevator, I brushed past a tiny man I recognized immediately. It's hard not to recognize Ramon Famosa's father/interpreter, Don Guardo! He seemed even cooler in person than on TV! He was wearing a plum-colored suit with matching hat. It had a bright orange feather in it, and his plump jaws worked over a slobbery cigar. He was heading outside, apparently to smoke. He talked into his cell phone as he did. I tried to get him to stop and talk to me, or at least pose for a picture, but he brushed past us. I had a video camera with me, of course, so I turned it on and aimed it directly at him. I had always wanted a video camera that looks like a pen, but no one ever bought me one. That would *so* be the kind of camera that a spy would have. Instead, mine was just a regular small cam. It's tiny, but it has a pretty good zoom. Don Guardo couldn't see me pointing it at him. He didn't stop talking. Probably he figured that I wouldn't understand what he was saying. Which, okay, I didn't. I didn't figure it out until later, but what he said was this: "*O, sí, estoy tan ocupado. He-he-he. Mi hermano— Lo siento— Señor Famosa no me necesita para nada. ¡Estúpido!*"

I had no idea what he was talking about. Man, I wished I had paid attention in Spanish class! Why did Señora Cohan have to be so boring?

Don Guardo Famosa was gone in a blur of purple, and the security guard led me and Dad up toward the announcers' booth. Even though I wasn't supposed to announce until the sixth inning, I got to hang out in the announcers' area the whole time. Dad would have to wait outside once the game started, but he walked in with me to meet the guys.

It was surprisingly small, a cramped little booth filled with microphones and cords and computers and hundreds of sheets of paper. There was barely enough room to walk around, yet so much to take in. The view of the ballpark was fantastic from the window in front. A huge panorama of bright green unfolded before me. It was enormous, like staring at the sun. Then the announcers walked in. Play-by-play guy Arnie Mickel stepped into the booth. He was a tall man with a friendly smile and a gleaming bald head—even balder than my father's, which I didn't know was possible. He extended his hand to mine. "Is this the kid who's gonna take my job?" he said with a laugh. "Hey, kid, you nervous? You know this broadcast goes not just into the city but through a considerable part of Pennsylvania. *And* parts of New Jersey."

"Well, hello, uh, Mick," I said, venturing his nickname. "I'm a little nervous, I guess."

He narrowed his eyes and formed his lips into a vicious sneer. "You call me Mr. *Mickel*," he said, eyes turning angry.

"Yeah," said Chuck Stockwell, one of the other announcers, sticking his head into the room. "You have to earn Mick-rights, kid."

Then Buck Foltz entered. "And if you even dream of calling me anything other than Mr. Foltz, you will find yourself dangling from this booth by your ankles, kiddo!"

"I—I—I—I'm sorry," I stammered. "I was just—"

Then they all started cracking up and high-fiving.

"We're only messing with you," Arnie said. "Just some announcer hazing. You can totally call me Mick."

"I thought we were being serious," Buck said, frowning. "I seriously will kill you if you don't call me Mr. Foltz."

Chuck Stockwell rolled his eyes. In the back of my mind, I heard the *wah-wah* of a sad trombone. It was going to be an interesting night.

I stared at Buck. He looked like a robot or a wax statue. When I thought about how many millions of people around the world knew that voice, I felt almost woozy to be so close to its source. Maybe *that's* why he looked unreal to me. I noticed Buck's Phillies shirt and the Phillies logo on his pants. I briefly wondered if he owned any non-Phillies clothing and concluded that he probably didn't. Phillies socks, Phillies undershirts, Phillies boxer shorts, and formal Phillies bow ties for weddings and funerals.

"Hey, kid," Mick said, slapping me on the shoulder and snapping me back to my surroundings. "Great work digging up that Blaze O'Farrell story. I know my Phils, but even I didn't realize we had the record for worst ERA ever. Go figure!"

"Yeah!" I said.

"And get this," he said. "The brass invited Blaze to come tonight!"

"Oh, I don't think he'll come," I said quickly.

"He's crazy! Totally nuts. He never leaves his house! He's a hermit!" Visions of flying bottles passed before my eyes, and I felt like I had to pee.

"Shows what you know, kid," he said. "He's down there on the field right now. They made him a coach for the day. He gets one more shot to put on a Phillies uniform. Gets to be right there in the dugout again! Let's hope he's not bad luck!"

Mick gestured toward a screen showing the on-field pregame warm-ups. An ancient little man in a Phillies jacket stood on the grass watching the pitchers. He looked angry. That was Blaze all right. His jaw was clenched tight, and his eyebrows were pointed down in an irritated squint, his skin so pale he almost looked like a ghost. The only physical characteristic that would ever have made you think that he was once a ballplayer was his hands. They were basically just normal hands, but huge. His fingers were enormous—like a fan of five magic wands. It made you wonder how he ever fit a glove on and why he wasn't able to do amazing things on the mound.

"Can I go down to see the dugout and the players and everything?" I asked. I wasn't anxious to run into Blaze again, but I had to ask.

"I don't think so, kid," Mick said. "Not on

game day. The booth is where the action is, anyway. It was my dream to be an announcer too. As you can see, sometimes dreams come true."

"Well, it was my dream to not have to work with dorks like you," Chuck said, elbowing Arnie and snickering. "So sometimes dreams do *not* come true."

I couldn't believe it. They were just like regular guys. Like me and the Mikes, only . . . older.

Buck seemed clueless. He was eating cottage cheese with a plastic spork. I was both impressed and appalled. He dribbled some on his chin.

"I know you're bummed you can't go down and meet the players," Chuck said. "But we got something pretty great for you." He pressed a button on an intercom on the wall of the cramped booth. "Hey, Gary, send in the kid," he said. "No, the other kid."

Another kid? I had no idea what he meant. In a few seconds, it was clear. The other kid was R. J. Weathers himself. Only he didn't look like a kid. I knew he was young—just nineteen. He was one of the youngest players since Putsy Caballero to make the Phils. But he looked enormous. I had to crane my neck up to see him. Longish brown hair was trying to escape from under his bright red hat, and his arms were at once skinny yet powerful, like coiled snakes under his sleeves. He was already in uniform and had a baseball in his hand. He furiously worked a piece of gum. Even his jaw muscles looked strong.

"Whoa!" I said. "R. J. Weathers! So cool to meet you, uh, sir." Everyone laughed.

"Nice to meet you," he said. "You a ballplayer yourself?"

"I was once, sir," I said. "I was the worst there ever was. . . ."

He ignored the second part of my sentence and said, "You don't have to call me sir." He talked in a slow, drawling voice. "Call me RJ."

"Yeah," Chuck said. "He's no sir. You two are probably about the same age."

"I'm only twelve," I said.

"Exactly," Chuck said, pointing with his thumb. "Him too." Everyone laughed again.

"Well, I'd love to sit here and listen to these jerks rip on me all night," RJ said with a smile. "But I got a game to win."

"Is that a promise?" Arnie asked.

"I don't make no promises," RJ said. "Other than to do my best. Oh, and congrats on winning the contest, kid. Here, take this." He tossed me a ball. And I caught it! It was covered in scribbles. "Everyone on the team signed it," he said.

"Even Famosa?" I asked in disbelief.

Everyone laughed again. I guess it was unexpected that Famosa, the error-prone backup catcher, was my favorite player.

"Sure thing, kid," RJ said, waving good-bye.

I didn't even get a chance to say thanks. Dad jumped in. I'd almost forgotten he was there. "Let's get something to eat before game time, Lenny," he said, looking at his watch. I wanted to keep hanging out with the crew. And I couldn't think about eating. The mere idea of ballpark nachos was about as appetizing to me as a plate of vomit.

But Dad insisted, so I picked at a slice of pizza. The butterflies in my stomach were fierce. I paced around the maroon-carpeted hallway outside the booth, anxious for the game to begin. This was worse than filming the Blaze O'Farrell thing—at least for that I had lines to memorize. I was going to have to be quick and funny on the fly. Could I do it? Would I freak out and accidentally go back to using the 1940s lingo, like I did for the video? Hi-de-ho I hoped not.

I couldn't believe that I had to wait until the

sixth before I could take the mike. My mind was going crazy imagining the ways I'd fail. I also couldn't help thinking about PhilzFan1, for some reason. I looked out over the swirling crowd. Was he there in the stands somewhere? Would he really take drastic action someday? Were fans really that crazy? Was gambling involved? I'd read a book about the 1919 World Series, when gamblers bribed players to throw the games. Unbelievable.

Then I thought about the Mikes. I wished they were here. They'd thought about trying to get tickets, but I told them to stay at home. What would be the point of being in the ballpark? They couldn't hear my announcing. It would be better if they had the TV on. It made me smile like crazy to picture them out on the lawn couch, tuning in to hear not Buck Foltz but Lenny Norbeck announce the game. Plus, yeah, maybe I didn't want them there in case I got nervous and peed myself.

The rest was a jittery blur. It all ran together: national anthem, starting lineups, cheer, boo, cheer. Finally, the game started. I was really happy to have something to concentrate on. I watched from the press section, where I sat next to newspaper reporters scribbling notes. It looked like a perfect life, but none of them appeared to realize that they had the greatest job in the world. They all looked a little grumpy and seemed to resent my being there. I tried to stay out of the way and ended up sitting in the back. I couldn't really see the field through the window, so I just watched it on one of the many TV screens.

The crowd gave a great roaring ovation for R. J. Weathers when he walked onto the field in the top of the first. Camera flashes exploded in the stands. If he ended up being the next Steve Carlton or Roy Halladay, people wanted proof that they were there on day one. So much hope in this young arm. He really was an impressive figure out there. His hair was hanging out of the back of his red cap and his apelike arms seemed to scrape the ground as he walked. He kissed his lucky necklace before tucking it into his uniform jersey. He took the mound.

And he was *terrible*. He threw everything but strikes. Walks, wild pitches, singles, and doubles. He hit a guy in the foot. He hit a guy in the shoulder. He hit a guy in the front row. He threw a pitch that landed closer to me in the announcer's booth than to the catcher. He hit a guy on the Giants (we were not playing the Giants—they were in

California, about three thousand miles away). Okay, slight exaggeration, but his pitches were just absolutely awful. The umpire didn't even bother to say "Ball" on a few of them. He just laughed. Loudly.

Philadelphia crowds can turn tough quickly, and they were booing Weathers before he got a single out. Someone held up a sign: TONIGHT'S FORECAST: BAD WEATHERS. I'd say so. It was mean, but a little funny. Pretty good pun. It was also impressive that they guessed he'd have a bad game. Or did they bring markers and create it on the spot? Some fans are crazy, but you sort of do have to admire their dedication and abilities at arts and crafts.

I felt bad for RJ. He was such a nice guy. But even great players have bad games, and surely his next one would be better. Maybe he was just nervous, like I was.

Pretty soon, home plate was turning into the finish line at the New York City Marathon. Runner after runner crossed home. There was a bases-clearing home run. It was 8–0 before RJ finally got one out on a pop-up that Famosa snagged (just barely) by the Phillies dugout. Then another walk.

The Phillies manager went out to the mound.

The trainer came out too. I didn't think there was anything physically wrong with Weathers, was there? Maybe he was injured. Maybe that explained it all. Or maybe they were just pretending he was hurt, as an excuse to save face. They brought him a water bottle and tried to settle him down. They rubbed his arm. They tugged on his elbow. Eventually, the umpire came out to break up the conference. The manager and trainer headed back toward the dugout. It seemed like they were going to leave Weathers in the game, let him try to get a few more outs.

But as soon as the trainer made it to the dugout, he had to sprint right back onto the field. R. J. Weathers had collapsed behind the mound. He just toppled over, like an invisible hand had punched him in the face and knocked him out cold. Like he was shot.

There was no blood, at least not that I could see. I craned my neck but couldn't get a better look. All the press guys were standing up—I could mostly just see their sweaty backs. I peeked through and saw that the trainer had been joined by paramedics and the team doctor and a whole crowd of people.

It was chaos in the press booth. The tired men

with their pens looked suddenly alive. They were scribbling as fast as they could. They were taking pictures. Papers were flying, flashes were flaring. Word came quickly to the booth: R. J. Weathers was dead.

CHAPTER SEVEN

The PA announcer's voice came over the speakers: "Tonight's game is officially canceled. Your tickets will be honored at a later date." That normally cheery booming voice that announces the starting lineups and pitching changes sounded so strange. The words sounded like they were getting stuck in his throat. He was choked up with emotion.

As we made our way out, I noticed lots of people who looked like they were going to cry. It was like a birthday party that had suddenly turned into a funeral. No one knew how to act. It was still early—not even eight. The sun had just set, turning the sky from blue to red. There were streaks of particularly dark red shooting over the park. I started having crazy thoughts, thinking these scarlet streaks were trails left behind every time a Phillie ascended to heaven. I felt my own eyes begin to flood with tears. I tried to wipe them on my shoulder without Dad seeing.

"At least we'll beat most of the traffic," Dad said. This was probably the dumbest thing anyone had ever said.

"Sure," I said. "That's just great." I know I sounded mad.

"I'm sorry, Lenny," Dad said. "I know you really wanted to do the inning. But I bet they'll invite you back. They have to."

They *didn't* have to. No one bothered to explain to me what to expect, and I didn't bother to ask because I felt like an idiot and didn't know who to ask, anyway. The guy who had led us into the booth was nowhere to be seen, and I couldn't exactly ask Mick or Foltz. Everyone had other things on their mind. My big chance was ruined. The boy with the golden voice would never take over the baseball world now. Didn't Dad see? I bit my lip as we pulled out of the parking lot. Then I felt bad. It could have been worse. I could have been R. J. Weathers.

Weathers was only a few years older than me, really. A kid. That's what they kept calling him. "A kid" with a bright future. "A kid" with an amazing arm. "A kid" who was now dead.

What had caused the sudden death of this rising star? How could someone so young die so unexpectedly? All I could think about was PhilzFan1, his typed words now so menacing. *Drastic action.* Murder? I laughed off the thought.

Dad must have been thinking something along the same lines—not about PhilzFan1 but about how Weathers was so young. "I can't fathom how his parents must feel," he said.

We sat in traffic, which really was quite bad. I told you what Dad said was dumb. The freeway was like a parking lot. We called Mom to check in.

"Are you okay, Lenny?" she asked me. "I was watching the game. So terrible."

"I'm fine," I said. "It's not like I was the one on the mound."

"No," she said. "But I know you've been looking forward to this so much."

A few tears came to my eyes—for my lost opportunity, sure, but more for RJ. "Thanks, Mom," I said. "Yeah."

I didn't say anything else. I *couldn't* say anything else. I didn't want to start bawling. "Thanks, Mom," I said again. "Do you want to talk to Dad?" I asked.

"No, that's fine, dear," she said. "I'll see you when you get home."

Then it got quiet. Just the soft hum of Dad's car and the honks of impatient drivers. I wanted to text the Mikes, to see what they had to say about this amazing turn of events. But of course I didn't have my phone.

"Can I use your phone to send a text, Dad?" I asked.

"This is my phone for work," he said. "You can't use it to text the Mikes a million times."

"Can you at least put on sports radio?" I said. "I want to hear WPP, see what they're saying about the game."

"All right," Dad said. "But if that loudmouth hillbilly is on, I'm turning it off."

You might think it's mean that Dad called the sports talk DJ a hillbilly, but that's actually what the DJ called himself. His full name was Billy Zabrowski or something, but he called himself "the Philly Hillbilly." That's what everyone else called him too. He was loud and tended to be pretty angry about sports, even when the Philly teams were winning. He was known for his tirades against coaches and players, and sometimes you could hear him smashing stuff in the studio.

Dad pressed the button to switch on the AM station. It was, in fact, Billy who was on, but he wasn't angry. He didn't sound like himself. He sounded really shaken up. He talked quieter than usual and in a serious voice.

"This is a tragedy tonight, folks. A young man cut down in the summer of his youth. A brilliant young arm with a future as bright as the sun. Dead. At nineteen. I'll take your calls tonight, but I'll warn you, if you make jokes out of this, if you have a laugh at the passing of this young lion, R. J. Weathers, I will not only hang up on you, I will come to your house and shove the phone—"

Dad pressed the Off button.

"Dad!" I yelled.

"Son," he said, "I do not want you listening to this kind of junk. The manners on that guy!"

"I thought what he said was nice," I said. "He felt bad about Weathers's death."

"Well, he certainly expressed it in a crude way."

"Just turn it back on, please?"

Dad relented. A caller was talking, his voice cracking over the airwaves. He was trying to sound all medical, but you could tell he didn't really know what he was talking about. "You know that the docs are gonna cover it up and say heart attack, but I've been reading scouting reports on this kid since he was in diapers. Nothing about a heart condition nowhere. You don't just croak at his age with no previous heart condition."

Dad turned up the radio. He wanted to hear more about the medical part. He was a heart specialist, after all. Sometimes, when I was feeling really sorry for myself, I'd think about how messed up it was that my dad was an expert on the heart, since I wasn't sure he even had one. Poor Lenny. Wah-wah.

"It really is quite rare for a young healthy man to suffer a heart attack like that," Dad said, talking over the radio. "I'd love to see the autopsy reports." He got carried away talking about things like EKGs and autopsies and aortic valve displacements. He didn't even seem to be talking *to* me—just near me. This is what it was always like with me and my dad. I found myself wishing Mike's dad was here. He'd let me use his phone. He'd be cooler about everything. Plus, he'd have some good snacks.

Then a classic loudmouth on the radio called in and started yelling about how there was only one explanation for what happened: drugs.

"I can't see anything except for drugs making his heart stop outta nowhere, know what I mean? Din't you see how he was pitching? Couldn't find the plate if it was the side of a freaking barn."

Billy didn't make good on his threat. He let the guy talk. Great. They were talking about how RJ's control was bad, not focusing on the fact that he was dead! It occurred to me that maybe these sports fans had a problem with priorities. It hurts me to say this, but there are things more important in life than throwing balls and strikes.

"What do you think, Dad?" I asked. "Could someone's heart just stop beating like that?"

"Well, stranger things have happened," he said. "But first, I'd like to take a look at the tox report. See if they find something fishy in his blood. You know: drugs."

It didn't seem right to me. "I only met him for a minute, but he seemed like such a good dude. I can't imagine he was on drugs."

"Well, it could have been any number of substances."

"You mean like steroids?" I had read all about how baseball players sometimes took drugs to make themselves stronger, but RJ definitely didn't have the look of the giant-head muscle-bound freaks from the Barry Bonds days. He was tall and lanky. And so kind.

"Could be, could be," Dad said. "It would be interesting to see the report. And then, of course, there will be an autopsy to take a look at his heart."

"Is an autopsy what I think it is?" I'm really not cut out to be a doctor because the thought of R. J. Weathers—anyone, really—getting sliced open so doctors can look at their heart makes me want to barf.

"Yes, well, they will want to look at his heart and other organs."

"I'm just going to pretend you mean with X-rays."

"The human body is really quite fascinating, Lenny. Nothing to be disturbed by."

"If you say so, Dr. Norbeck," I said. We were quiet for a second. Then I had a thought. "Hey, you don't think they'll do the autopsy at *your* hospital, do you? Will you get to see the report or whatever?"

"No, probably not. There's a hospital in Center City—much closer to the ballpark than mine. I'm pretty sure that's where they'll take him."

"Do you think you still could get a copy of the report?"

"Maybe. I know some docs over there. Why?"

"I just . . . I just want to know how he died."

I had a spooky feeling I couldn't explain. Maybe it was the shock of coming so close to death. Maybe it was superstition and nerves. Maybe it was just fear. Or maybe something sinister happened on that field. Was PhilzFan1 a harmless blowhard on the Internet? Or did he have something to do with it? Nah, he couldn't have gotten into the dugout and poisoned RJ. It was crazy. But something felt so . . . off. Then I thought about RJ giving me the ball with the team's signatures, and I felt incredibly sad.

"I just want to know," I said. Dad seemed proud. Maybe he thought I was coming around on the whole "the human body is an amazing spectacle" attitude or whatever. Really, I just wanted to know if there was any chance it was murder.

"It *is* a strange case," Dad said. "I'll give you that."

Traffic had finally broken. I could see the spire of the Schwenkfelder Church. We were close to home.

"Can you drop me off at Mike's?" I asked.

"I don't know, Leonard," Dad said. "I realize it's been a rough night and you'd like to talk to your friend, but it's getting late."

"It's not that late," I said. "And it's not like it's a school night."

"School night or not, it's too late for you to be out," he said. "You'll talk to the Mikes in the morning."

"I'll talk to the Mikes tonight," I muttered under my breath. "Whether you like it or not."

Dad swung the car into the garage and we headed in to see Mom. She was sitting in front of the TV.

"Oh, Lenny," she said. "I'm so sorry about what happened." Was she upset about me not getting to do my inning or about Weathers? I really didn't care about the inning anymore, and I'm not just saying that. Sure, it was my dream or whatever, but now bigger stuff was happening! More important stuff. Plus, it felt so out of the ordinary that she cared all of a sudden. Is that what it takes? I had to witness a murder before she remembered I was alive?

"I've been watching the news," Mom said. "It's on all the channels. Come join me." She patted the spot next to her on the couch. "Did you eat? I can make you something." I *was* pretty hungry.

I plopped down on the couch and watched the TV footage showing RJ dropping to the ground. The reporter was very serious and very sad. He used the word *tragedy* a whole bunch of times, as did everyone he talked to. If I had to sum up the coverage, it would be that people thought it was an enormous tragedy that this tragedy had tragedied the tragedy of this great tragedy city. Tragedy.

Then the reporter said that no foul play was suspected. I snorted and it must have been a loud snort. Because Mom, who was returning to the living room with what appeared to be a pretty sweet-looking PB&J, heard me. It was the heart-healthy kind of peanut butter, of course, which kind of tastes a little like paste, but I was too distracted to complain.

"What are you snorting for?" Mom asked, pointing to the somber-looking newscaster. "You don't believe what the reporter said?"

Why *didn't* I believe him? Maybe it's just because I felt like Tom Thomas or whatever dumb fake name the reporter made up for himself didn't know the whole story. He didn't know about the rabid maniacs like PhilzFan1. I knew that if I wanted to get the true story on what had happened, I'd have to go to the Internet. It sucked so bad to be banned from the computer! It was password-protected and basically under lock and key. They did let me keep my phone, but only during the day. It was the worst grounding ever. I thought they might give in if I played up the "poor Lenny" angle tonight.

I took a bite of the sandwich and blurted out "Can I use the computer?" through a mouthful of sticky peanut butter. "I want to see what they're saying about the game online. And chat with the Mikes maybe. Nothing else. I swear!"

"You know you aren't allowed on the computer until school starts again."

"This is a special occasion!"

She seemed to think about it for a second, but then she declared, "Rules are rules." This is one of her favorite statements despite the fact that it doesn't mean anything. Of course rules are rules. What else would they be? What can you say to someone whose big argument is that a thing is itself? That rules are actually *not* rules? That they're what, then? Elves? "No, Mom. Rules are, in fact, elves." Yeah. So I said nothing and kept chewing.

"Besides," she said, "I'm sure they're saying the same exact things. You can get all the news you need here." She was so wrong. The news on TV *wasn't* the same thing. I had to get online, see what the real fans were saying. I had to get to Bedrosian's Beard. To see what PhilzFan1 was saying.

"I'm just going to go to bed early," I said. She

looked disappointed. Why did she want to hang out all of a sudden? I felt a little guilty not spending time with her. She was being nice. It was odd. And sort of sweet—she never really had time to spend with me. But at this particular moment, I had other things to do. I had a death to investigate. I owed it to RJ to find out the truth.

I went to my room and fell into bed without getting changed. I lay there in the dark, trying to sleep, but questions were zooming through my mind like fastballs crossing the plate. *Zoom!* Did R. J. Weathers really have a heart attack? *Whoosh!* Is that possible for someone so young and so healthy? *Whiz!* Could it be possible that he was killed? *Zip!* Was that crazy PhilzFan1 somehow involved? I just knew something was up. But what? Gambling? Stalkers? All I wanted was to talk to the Mikes and see what the Internet had to say. How was I going to sleep? How was I going to lie there while RJ's killer was possibly gloating online?

I felt like a star player on the disabled list when he was needed for a clutch at bat. Like how the Phils' best hitter, Rafael Boyar, was on the bench for tonight's game. I really wanted to talk about this whole thing with the Mikes! And to use Mike's computer! But how would I get over there?

Thank you, Blaze O'Farrell. The hidden-ball trick! The hidden-ball trick is all about being two places at once. The ball *appears* to be in the pitcher's glove when it actually is in the glove of the other player. Misdirection. All I had to do was appear to be in my bed while actually being somewhere else.

I carefully crafted a fake Lenny under the sheets. I really did a good job, using a bunch of other shirts to fill out my pajama shirt and two pillows carefully positioned to look like legs. I even topped it off with a bit of Fuzzy Monkey above the covers, since Fuzzy had the same color hair as me. (Wait. Did I just admit that I still have stuffed animals? *Whoops. Never mind. Moving on.*) I stepped back to admire my handiwork. It looked pretty good. Hidden-ball-trick good.

The next thing I had to do was to get my phone. It was confiscated each night, but I knew where my parents kept it. I just hoped I could get it from Dad's nightstand without waking Mom or him up. I waited, lying in bed beside the fake Lenny until my Phillies clock blinked a red 11:00. I fell asleep a bunch of times but woke up with bad dreams of a grinning PhilzFan1. (This was weird, because I had no idea what he looked like.)

Once it was eleven o'clock, I figured it was safe to sneak into the parents' room and grab the phone. As quietly as an expert base stealer leading off first, I crept out of my room and down the dark hall. I heard the buzz-saw sound of Dad's epic snore from the bedroom and knew I was safe. I held my breath and turned the doorknob. It gave the slightest creak, and I heard my parents rustling in their bed. I quickly darted back around the corner. My heart was pounding in my chest and I started to sweat. But it seemed like they were still asleep.

We had lived in this house my whole life, and I knew where everything was like a veteran outfielder knows the nooks and crannies of his home stadium. I crawled—literally, crawled like a baby—across the floor. I found my way to Dad's nightstand. I closed my eyes tight, like this might make me invisible. It didn't matter if my eyes were open or closed. Either way it was the same—total darkness. Slowly, I opened the top drawer.

And then Dad sat up and screamed. "Ahhhh!"

CHAPTER EIGHT

I knew I was caught.

Grounded. Supergrounded. Not just from the phone and the computer. From the Mikes. From the outside world. From life. Forever.

I dived under the bed like a runner scrambling back to beat the tag at first base on a pickoff throw. I lay there, my face inches from the bedsprings. The side my mom was on almost reached the ground. It smelled just awful under there. I tried to inch over, but I was blocked in. My hand pressed against something hard and cool. *What is it?* My fingers found a grooved circular piece in the middle. I turned it and immediately recognized the sound. It sounded just like the lockers at school. A combination lock. *Why does Dad have a locked metal box under his bed?*

I was sure that the next thing I heard would

be Dad's voice saying "What was that noise?" From there he would of course check my room, and only an idiot would fall for my hidden-ball trick with Fuzzy Monkey. Who did I think I was fooling?

But the next thing I heard was Mom's voice. Talking to Dad.

"Bad dreams again, Jeff?"

"Mr. Rucker's heart stopped! Get the paddles!"

"You're at home, Jeff," she calmly said. "You're just having a bad dream."

"Where am I?" Dad asked in a groggy voice.

"You're at home, Jeff," she said. "I'm here. It's okay."

"Mr. Rucker . . . ," Dad said.

"Mr. Rucker is in a better place, Jeff," Mom said. I had the strong feeling that I shouldn't be hearing this. Who was Mr. Rucker? A patient of Dad's? Did something bad happen at work? Did Dad have to deal with people dying all the time? Was that why he wasn't too upset about R. J. Weathers? Maybe that was his life—someone dies and you just get on with your day. You hope traffic isn't too bad. Why didn't he ever talk about this kind of stuff? I wouldn't mind listening. I made a mental note to ask him, if I made it out from under that bed alive. I also made a note to figure out what locked secrets he had in that box.

"Mr. Rucker . . . ," Dad said again, muttering. "Mr. Rucker . . ." And then he must have fallen back asleep because his snore picked up right where he had left off, sawing logs like an industrial chain saw. I wished I could tell if Mom was asleep or not, but I had no such clear signal. I decided to wait a few minutes. My thoughts were a scary jumble of Mr. Rucker and R. J. Weathers and Philz-Fan1. Once it seemed safe, I crawled out from under the bed, scooting softly across the floor.

The snoring continued. I seemed safe. I stayed low, arching my back to reach into the open nightstand while remaining out of view. My hand found the familiar form of my phone and I crawled backward, softly closing the door behind me. I stopped in the bathroom just so I'd have an excuse for the noise if they woke up. I looked at myself in the mirror. My face was white. Like I'd seen a ghost. I glanced at the phone. There were a bunch of texts waiting for me—including one from Mike just a few minutes ago.

r u up?

I wrote back:

of course! u?

I didn't feel like trying to explain it all through texting, so I kept it simple:

i m coming over

He texted a quick response:

window in back

I knew what I had to do.

I'd never sneaked out of the house before, but I had spent a lot of time thinking about it. Mainly in little-kid daydreams about what I'd do if there was a fire or a burglar in the house. The way I always knew I'd do it was simple: garage window. It was the only window in the house that didn't have a screen. It was almost always closed and locked, but it was easy to open from the inside. You just had to pop a lock, climb on the seat of the lawn mower, and hop out. I had actually tried it a few times when I was younger, practicing escaping from burglars, I guess. I always pictured them wearing those black masks that cover just the top part of your face. I was weird when I was little. . . .

The first step was just to get down to the garage. Again, I felt like a base runner trying to steal second. There was an area of safety where you knew you could always get back to first. If I was in the living room and Mom woke up, I could say I couldn't sleep. But there always had to be that point. The point of no return. You could no longer scamper back to the base, you just had to put your head down and go, go, go.

I figured the point of no return was pretty much the threshold to the garage. I could always claim that I was downstairs for some reason or other, but why would I be in the garage after eleven o'clock at night? Once I stepped onto the concrete, I'd just have to run. I took a deep breath and did exactly that. I hopped through the door to the garage, hustled through the darkness to the window, popped it open, and squeezed out. I didn't get stuck. I was free. I was in the night. I was running. I was rounding the bases. Except that I wasn't headed for home. I was leaving it.

Mike's house wasn't too far by bike, but it took forever to run there. I felt so suspicious-looking, sprinting down the dark streets. I was sure that a cop would stop to pick me up or a nosy neighbor would bust me. But there was no turning around. I just put my head down and sprinted as fast as I could until my legs burned and my heart felt like it was going to explode. I was like a slow, old backup catcher trying for an inside-the-park home run. It was just too much running.

I made it to Mike's house around midnight. The back window to his basement lair was open, just as he said it would be. I poked my head in and saw him sitting there, organizing his cards, memorizing the facts on the back. I was never so happy to see anyone in my life. Before I even said a word, he hissed, "Keep it down." I guess my breathing was pretty loud.

"I ran . . . *gasp* . . . the whole . . . *gasp* . . . way," I said, trying to whisper. We had to keep quiet so his parents wouldn't hear us.

"I wouldn't have guessed," he said. "From the way you're sweating and panting, I would have guessed you caught a ride over in your air-conditioned limo." Normally he'd laugh at his own joke, but his face was dead serious. His brown eyes looked almost black.

"Yeah," I said, still gasping. "Good one."

"So what the heck happened? I can't believe your inning got canceled! Did you get to meet anyone? Do you think they'll have you back?"

"Who cares about my inning?" I said. "Weathers is dead!"

"I know, I know, I know," Mike said. "It's so messed up."

"Are you thinking what I'm thinking?" I said excitedly.

Mike, apparently, was not. "Um, that the Phils are really going to have to make a trade for some pitching now?"

"What?" I said. "No!"

"Well, we really do need some more pitching if we're going to—"

"Mike," I said, looking him straight in the eyes, "I don't think RJ just died randomly. He looked totally fine when I saw him."

"Whoa, you met him?" Mike said, his voice excited and a little bit jealous. "Famosa too?"

"No, only RJ came up to the booth. I did run into Don Guardo, though. I recorded him talking. But it's Spanish. I have no idea what he was saying."

"Señora Cohan would be so disappointed," Mike said.

"Yeah," I said, managing a laugh. "But, seriously—we need to find more out about what happened tonight. Something definitely went down. My dad thought so too. Well, he didn't exactly say it, but he did say it was an odd case. And that he'll try to get the report from the hospital. If it turns out that this was no accident . . . If someone did this to RJ, we know just who to look for."

"Who?" he asked.

"PhilzFan1!" I said. "It's gotta be . . . right?"

"What? You really think that turd is in on this?" Mike said. He shook the mouse to wake up his computer. The Bedrosian's Beard website appeared on the screen. The light cast an eerie glare through the dark basement. It was extremely late, but I felt very much awake. "I know he did say something about 'drastic measures,' but this is, like, really drastic."

"Let me on there," I said.

"No one touches my computer but me," he said. "Don't you see the sign?" He pointed to a sign he'd obviously typed up on said computer and printed out. In big, bold letters, it read: THIS COMPUTER IS FOR THE HANDS OF MICHAEL ANTHONY DINUZZO ONLY. VIOLATORS WILL BE EATEN BY A RABID YAK. Then there was a picture of an angry yak.

"I thought that was just to keep Arianna away." Her irrational fear of yaks was well known, the result of a zoo trip gone bad.

"I'd love to help you out, Leonard," Mike said. "But that yak is pretty dangerous."

I rolled my eyes. "Fine. You read it. Just tell me what it says, will ya?"

"Lots and lots of posts tonight," he said, cracking his knuckles.

"I bet."

"Lots of theories about how Weathers died. Drugs. Heart attack. Here's one that mentions poison!"

"Whoa! PhilzFan1?"

"Nah," Mike said. "Some guy named BigJeltz-Machine posted it. He said that Weathers probably poisoned himself to avoid hearing the Philly Hillbilly rip him in the morning. It has lots of smileys after it. I guess he was just joking."

"Why do people keep joking? It's really not funny!" I felt myself getting angry. "I know we just talked for a minute, but R. J. Weathers was the only ballplayer I've ever met. He was so cool. And now he's gone?"

"Keep your voice down," Mike said. "If my parents wake up, you're dead. Arianna's room is right up there. She lives for getting me in trouble. It's, like, her favorite hobby. She does two things—she collects glass unicorns and she gets me in trouble. This is what she does. Plus, she hates you."

"Why does she hate me so much?"

"I don't know, Lenny. She's nine. Who knows why she does anything? Glass unicorns?"

Mike scrolled through the pages and pages of posts. "Nothing new from PhilzFan1," he said with a shrug. "His last post was early this morning. Yesterday morning, I mean. Man, it's late! We better not get caught."

I checked the clock. Way past bedtime. Normally I'd be snoozing happily, dreaming of bunting my way on base. (Is it weird that in my dreams I'm always bunting for a hit instead of hitting a home run? Don't answer that.) But even though it was late, I had no desire for sleep.

"What did that last one say?" I asked, feeling my heart pound.

Mike read PhilzFan1's words out loud in a whisper: " 'I'm going to the game tonight. I got free tickets, so don't give me grief for breaking the boycott. It should be fun to watch Weathers suck with the force of a thousand vacuum cleaners. And if you watch closely, I'll have a little surprise in store for my followers. Stay tuned. Mwahahahahaha—' "

"A surprise in store? That's such a threat!" I said. "And he admitted that he was there tonight!" Could I really be onto something?

Mike continued, "Mwa ha. Ha. Ha. Ha."

"Are you done?" I asked.

Mike's mouth turned into a small smile. "He wrote *ha* a lot of times," he said.

"Yeah," I said. "I got that."

Mike went back to clicking the screen, scrolling and scrolling. "Man, there are a ton of posts tonight," he said. "It's flying by. Here's one you'll want me to read, I'm sure. It says, 'WHAT REALLY HAPPENED?' in all caps with a bunch of the words spelled wrong."

"What do they say really happened?"

"Well, someone on here said they followed the ambulance leaving the game."

"Why would they do that?"

"I don't know—people are nuts. Maybe they wanted a picture with Weathers."

"After he was dead?"

"More likely than asking for an autograph."

"I guess . . ."

"Anyway, it said that the ambulance passed Center City Hospital and then the guy lost him."

"Where was it going?"

"That's the question."

"There are a lot of questions," I said. "Don't you see, Mike? Something weird happened. What if PhilzFan1 killed R. J. Weathers?"

"Why? Because he had a bad game? And more importantly, *how*? RJ's heart stopped. You can't do that from the stands, no matter how good your seats are."

Mike had a point, but still. "The *why* is clearly because he was an insane stalker," I said. "Now, for the how—"

Then Mike's computer beeped. I almost jumped out of my skin. "Calm down, Lenny," he said. "I must have left a chat open from before. It's from Other Mike." I leaned over to read the screen, careful not to actually touch the computer. I'm sort of afraid of yaks too.

> **Other Mike:** Hear from Len?
> **Mike:** yeah, he's here.
>
> **Other Mike:** What? Having a sleepover without me? Jerks.
> **Mike:** nah, he just came over.
>
> **Other Mike:** It's superlate!
> **Mike:** what are you doing up so late yourself?
>
> **Other Mike:** Ah, can't sleep. Saw you were on.
> **Mike:** yeah, me & len are trying

to look up some stuff about
what happened tonight.

Other Mike: What happened?
Mike: you didn't hear? the
baseball game Len was supposed
to announce at? the pitcher
died.

I had to break in here. "Dude, what the heck? Other Mike wasn't even watching the game? Ask him why he missed my big inning!"

"He says he forgot," Mike said. "Probably got obsessed with the new *Warlock Wallop.*"

"Tell him he's a jerk," I said.

"Ah, tell him yourself," Mike said. "I'm tired of being your secretary. Just be careful with the computer."

"I knew the yak was only an empty threat!" I said.

Mike pushed the chair back and got up from the computer, rolling his eyes. "Wow, you are definitely a great detective. I don't really have a rabid yak in my house. How you figured that one out, the world will never know. You're, like, Norbeck Holmes." He lay down on the floor, looking like he might fall asleep. I was just getting started.

Me: hey, it's me, lenny.
Other Mike: I can't believe Mike's letting you use his computer!

Me: I know. this is a big day for us all.
Other Mike: It'll probably be your last day.

Me: the yak is just an empty threat. you might be right though. my parents will kill me if they found out i snuck out!
Other Mike: How'd you do that??

Me: hidden-ball-trick-style.
Other Mike: I have no idea what you're talking about.

Me: listen, I need your help with something on the computer. if I send you a link to a message board, can you figure out the identity of the person behind the screen name?
Other Mike: Uh, maybe?

Me: you don't sound very confident.

Other Mike: Well, it's hard.
People like to be anonymous
online. I could probably figure
out the IP address maybe?
That's like the identifying
address for any computer.
Doesn't always tell you who the
person is, but it's a start.
Send over what you have and
give me a minute.

I laughed and sent Other Mike the link to PhilzFan1's Bedrosian's Beard profile. "What are you laughing about?" Mike said from his spot on the floor.

"*IP address* is a funny computer term," I said. "It sounds like 'I pee.'"

"Sure does," Mike agreed. "What does it mean?"

I explained to him what Other Mike had said, that each computer on the Internet has its own address, called "I pee," for some reason. We made dumb jokes and laughed about that for a few minutes. Possibly we were getting delirious from exhaustion. Then the computer beeped again. Other Mike, coming through in the clutch!

Other Mike: Well, you're not
going to believe this.

Me: you got the name of the guy making those posts?!

Other Mike: No, but I do have the location.
Me: yeah? then we can just find out whose house that is and we're on our way!

Other Mike: Well, it's not a house.
Me: what then?

Other Mike: If I'm doing this correctly, and I always am, the person posting behind the name PhilzFan1 is doing so from a library.
Me: huh.

Other Mike: Not just any library.
Me: huh?

Other Mike: OUR library!

I let that sink in for a moment. I must have looked like I was in shock because Mike glanced up and said, "You okay, Len? You look like you saw a ghost."

"Get over here and read this," I hissed.

Mike looked at me, then at the screen, then back at me. "Whoa," he said.

Other Mike kept typing. He explained that if you checked the time on the post from yesterday, you could tell it was made really early in the morning. The library wasn't even open yet!

I looked at Mike. Mike looked at me. The cursor blinked. Other Mike was thinking too. It was a tense moment. But like a couple of teammates who've spent years playing next to each other, we each knew what the other was thinking without saying a word: *Who could possibly be in the library before it opens, unless they worked at the library?* I suddenly heard a voice from upstairs.

"Miiiiiiiiiike!" It was Arianna. "Who are you taaaaaalking tooooooooo?"

"Crap," Mike whispered to me. "You gotta get outta here." Then he called up to his sister. "It's just the TV, Ari," he said. "Go back to bed."

"I'm getting Mom!" she said.

I did a quick impression of a late-night infomercial so Ari would think I was the TV and nothing else. I adopted a corny talk-show voice and said, "For just three easy payments of fourteen ninety-five, you can have not one, not two, not three, but *four* thousand knives sharper than the teeth of an angry yak!"

"Good one," Mike whispered. He cracked a smile but wiped it away. "Don't make me laugh. You better go!" Then he called back up to his sister in a somewhat louder voice, still quiet enough not to wake his parents. Sort of a screaming whisper. I love the scream-whisper. "Don't bother Mom, Ari," he said. "I'll let you use the computer all day tomorrow." Then he turned to me and said in a real whisper, "I hate you, Leonard Norbeck." But he said it with a smile. "See you at the library first thing in the morning?"

"First thing," I said. "Tell Other Mike. Let's get there *before* they open so we can scout it. I'll bring the telescope."

"Of course you will," he said. "Of course."

I pounded his fist and darted toward the window. Out into the night. Rounding the bases. Heading home. I barely felt my feet move as I sprinted. I was carried by the wind and distracted by the new information. PhilzFan1 worked at the library? Who did we know that worked in the library and was a Phillies fan?

The only and obvious answer was Mr. Bonzer.

Was Mr. Bonzer really PhilzFan1? Did he spend his mornings before the library opened posting angry rants on the library's computer? And could he have been the one who had something to do with the death of R. J. Weathers? I kept asking myself these questions over and over again, like maybe I was hoping to come to a different conclusion. It's like when they show old ball games on TV during the winter and I watch them anyway and root for the good guys to win even when I know beyond a shadow of a doubt that they lose.

It made me feel uneasy, imagining this guy I talked to every day actually being a psycho stalker and a murderer. If Mr. Bonzer was PhilzFan1 and a murderer, could, I don't know, Mike's dad be a secret health food nut? Could my teachers all be hired assassins in the summers? Could Courtney the Caretaker have a double life as an ultimate fighter? I had to put aside this train of thought for a much more immediate concern: getting back into the house.

Getting out was one thing. By the time the parents heard the noise of me leaping out of the garage and then came to check whether I was in my room, they'd see "me" and go back to bed. They'd see hidden-ball-trick Lenny made out of pillows and shirts and Fuzzy Monkey. But if they heard a noise on my way back in? They'd bump into me in the hallway. It struck me that maybe the fake Lenny fooled no one, and they'd be waiting for me in the driveway. I'd be a dead duck—like when the ball arrives ten seconds before a runner tries to steal second and all he can do is hang his head and accept his fate. But if they woke up and found me missing, there would be some evidence. Right? There would be sirens and calls to the Mikes, right?

I approached my house, and for a second I barely recognized it. Had they done something to it in my absence? Impossible. I checked my cell. I had only been gone just over an hour and a half. Plus, it was the middle of the night. Had something in me shifted during that time? It seemed like everything was changing. Just the other day it seemed like the biggest thing in the world was winning this contest. Now there was a murder and I was sneaking out of the house and the whole world had gone crazy.

I had to use all the strength in my skinny arms to pull myself up through the window. Then I had to close the window, cross the dark garage, open a few doors, and get into my bed without arousing a slumbering cardiologist. These were all challenges, yes. But the weird thing is, I did it. Perfectly. I did it. I snuck out of the house. And back in. I put on my pajamas and got into bed. My heart was pounding in my throat, and for some reason I felt like I could taste blood. Yet my parents didn't wake up. I closed my eyes. And I didn't feel scared. I felt . . . happy? I knew it was wrong to feel happy, but this was way more exciting than just announcing an inning. This was big. I needed to dig deep, to honor R. J. Weathers's memory, and his family, and every great baseball player I admired who'd want to know the truth.

CHAPTER NINE

My Phillies alarm clock blared "Take Me Out to the Ball Game" at 7:43 a.m. After a few pounds of the old snooze bar, I was raring to go. Well, not quite raring . . .

The library opened at nine o'clock, but we wanted to be there *before* nine, if possible. Mom and Dad were already gone for work by the time I got out of bed. Courtney was there, hanging out inside, which probably meant it was going to rain. She was like a human weather report. She was baffled that I was up so early, but I told her that I wanted to get a jump on going to the library, which, technically, was true.

"Are you okay, Lenny?" she asked as I made my way into the kitchen. "You're acting weird even for you."

"What is that supposed to mean?" I asked,

quickly pouring myself a bowl of cereal. It was heart-healthy cereal, so it sort of tasted like Styrofoam packing peanuts, but I was in a hurry.

"I don't know," she said. "I hear you had a rough night."

"Yeah," I said. "You could say that." What did *she* know about it?

"Your dad was telling me a little about it before he left this morning," she said. "Oh, and he told me to give you this." She handed me a piece of paper folded in half. I opened it up. It was a printout of an email from one of Dad's doctor friends. The time stamp showed it was sent early this morning.

Hey, Dr. J—

Yeah, I was here when they brought the pitcher in, doing my night down in the ER. Not all of us get the sweet cardiologist hours. ☺

Anyway, yeah, it'll be some time until we get all the results back, of course, but I'll tell you what I saw: nothing. No signs of drugs,

no signs of trauma, no signs
of anything. I did my time
in sports medicine back in
college when steroids were
everywhere, and this guy
looked nothing like any of
those guys. The kid looked
like he died peacefully.
Like a healthy, normal kid
who just went to sleep.
Definitely weird. Definitely
suspicious circumstances.

I'm not saying it's foul
play, but I ain't ruling it
out. Looking pretty likely,
to tell you the truth. But
we'll get to the bottom of
it. I'll keep you posted. Why
do you ask? Thinking about
changing careers and becoming
a homicide detective? ☺

Probably goes without saying,
but don't repeat any of this.
The press is crawling all
over here and the hospital
is trying to keep everything
nice and private. ☺

Tell the missus hello. More
soon.

My first thought was: *Dad has a friend who teases
him and uses smileys in emails? And calls him "Dr. J"?
Weird.* My next thought was, of course, that this
was something huge. I was going to honor the doctor's wish to keep it out of the press, and certainly
wasn't going to blab to Bedrosian's Beard. But I *had*
to tell the Mikes! "Thanks," I said to Courtney
once I remembered my manners. I folded the paper up and stuck it in my pocket. *Wait until the guys
see this!*

As I rode to the library, I wondered what I
would find. Was I about to unmask PhilzFan1? It
wasn't just my mind playing tricks on me. Something fishy really did happen last night. RJ's death
wasn't from drugs, and it wasn't an accident. Even
to a doctor it seemed like a weird case. *Foul play.*
Was I about to solve a murder? Would the Mikes
even show up? Then I saw them and smiled. The
two of them were spinning around the parking lot
on their bikes. They were the best friends ever, but
terrible spies.

"Dudes," I said. "Don't be so obvious. This is
undercover work."

"Oh, right," Other Mike said. "Wait—why?"

"We're trying to catch a killer here. We don't want anyone to see us. Come on. I have a good spot in mind to set up the telescope."

"Hey, do you ever have the feeling that *we're* being watched?" Other Mike said. "I've had that weird feeling, like, all summer."

"No," I said. "Don't be ridiculous. We're the ones doing the snooping."

"I don't know," Other Mike said, whipping his head around nervously. "I feel like someone's watching us."

Hearing him say that made *me* feel nervous, and I started looking around too.

"Would you two shut up?" Mike said. "Not that it matters. We're too late." He sat on his bike, not going anywhere, just spinning the pedals with his feet. "Look," he said, pointing across the parking lot. "There are a few cars here already. If you were hoping to catch him walking in, it's probably too late."

"Yeah, *we* were here a half hour ago," Other Mike said.

"Snooze bar," I muttered. "It'll be the death of me. That's what Mom always says."

"She's onto something," Mike said.

"Well, who else could be in there?" I asked. "Besides Bonzer, I mean. A crazy janitor? Do libraries have janitors? Did you see anyone go in? What if a homeless person is living in the library?"

"Beats me. The cars were here before we were," Mike said with a shrug.

"There's always tomorrow," I said.

"As if you'll be up early tomorrow," Other Mike said. "That would be like a pitcher hitting a home run. Eh? Eh?" He smiled. Other Mike was always really proud of himself when he made a baseball reference. They didn't come naturally to him, so he liked to celebrate.

"Okay, change of plans," I said.

"How so?" Mike asked.

"The time has passed for observation," I said. "Now is the time for interrogation." It was something I had read in a spy book, and it sounded cool. The Mikes laughed, but they were willing to go along with the plan.

We waited for the library to open, and I marched right in to find Mr. Bonzer. The boys followed. Mr. Bonzer looked sinister sitting there at the desk. Like he *did* have it in him to be a killer. His teeth looked sharper and pointier than I remembered, like the teeth of a shark. Maybe it was just in my head. Like when you're in a bad mood and every song in the world seems like a sad song or when you're extremely tired and you see someone running and you can't fathom how or why it's possible to be in such a hurry.

I kept myself cool. I had to improvise. What do you do when you're behind the plate and your star pitcher doesn't have command of his best pitch that day? If he's known for his curve but his curve isn't working? You change it up. You call for the fastball. You roll with it. Just get him talking. See what he has to say.

I made that hand gesture that meant "Step aside, Mikes. The Lenmeister has got this one." It seemed like something a real detective would do. Um, right?

"Good morning, Mr. Bonzer," I said.

"Morning," he groaned, sipping from a bright red Phillies coffee mug.

"Tired?" I asked, narrowing my eyes a little. I was trying to seem tough and also to see if I could notice any other details around his desk. There wasn't much. It was a mess of papers—catalogs, envelopes, and of course a lot of books. Nothing *overtly* sinister, but you can never tell. I would have loved to get a look at his computer screen, but he kept it turned at an angle that made it impossible to see. Tell me *that's* not a bit sinister.

"Slightly tired, yes," Bonzer said, looking like he would never leave that chair. He was like a hibernating bear stuck in a cave. "I'll snap out of it soon." He held up his coffee mug. "Thanks for asking. How about you? You're up early. I've never seen you three here before noon."

"Well, I'm working on a, um, project," I said. "It's due tomorrow. I had to get an early start."

"What kind of project? More baseball research?"

"No, it's for . . . school."

"You are aware that it's summer vacation. Which makes it kind of unlikely that you have a school project due *tomorrow*. Just saying."

"It's summer school," I said.

"You go to summer school? At Schwenkfelder Middle? I was just there talking to the summer-school kids about the library. I didn't see you."

Why was he thwarting all my efforts? I was unthwartable!

"No, it's not real school. It's, um, like, something my parents make me do."

"Home heart surgery—stuff like that?"

"Hey, how did you know that my parents are

cardiologists?" (What I really wanted to ask was: *Are you a master spy?*)

"Small town, Leonard. There aren't a lot of Norbecks."

Why is he counting Norbecks?

"True that," I said, for some reason.

"So, what is this project you're working on? Something I can help you with?"

"It's actually about, um, libraries," I lied.

"Then I'm the man to ask, I suppose." He stroked his beard.

"Yes, well, see . . . my parents wanted me to learn more about a city institution or whatever, and I chose the library. I have a bunch of questions I need to have answered."

"Well, that's wonderful! A noble civic institution if there ever was one. Not that I'm biased. Do you have the questions with you?"

I patted myself down like I was looking for the paper. I looked like a confused coach unclear if I was telling someone to bunt or steal second.

"I forgot it?" was the brilliant excuse I came up with.

"Do you *remember* any of the questions?" he asked with a sigh. But a friendly sigh. He really was a nice guy. *Isn't he?*

I paused for a second and scratched my head. Why does head scratching equate to thinking? Monkeys are always scratching themselves, and I doubt they're thinking much of anything. Maybe about riding bikes. I saw a monkey riding a bike once at the circus. I wondered how they got a bike that small. *Focus, Leonard!*

Maybe I could lure Bonzer away from his desk and give Other Mike a chance to snoop around. With his computer skills, if he could get access to Bonzer's computer, he could find out for sure if his computer was the one with the IP address that matched the one we had for PhilzFan1!

But I knew there was no way Bonzer was going to move from that chair. There was a time for being subtle, and there was a time for being blunt. Isn't that what a real detective would do? Wait, why would I think I was a real detective? What was I doing?

"Is there anyone who might be using these computers before the library is open?" I said, trying to sound tough.

"Lenny, what is this about? I know you're not doing any project on libraries. I thought you were merely being nosy. But it's starting to sound like something is going on here. Just tell me."

How does he know?! What to do now?! Telling him does seem to be the only option.

"Okay, Mr. Bonzer," I said, lowering my voice to an even quieter hush than the normal library level. I also hoped the voice sounded very serious and important. "I'll level with you." I heard the Mikes snicker, but I pressed on.

"Please do," he said.

I don't think my voice conveyed the seriousness of the situation as well as I hoped because it sort of squeaked. Mr. Bonzer smiled, then wiped at his mouth to erase the grin. "I think someone has been sending messages from the library's computer to a baseball website. A Phillies website. Bedrosian's Beard. Do you know it?"

If he knew of the site, that would be a clue! Maybe Mr. Bonzer was PhilzFan1 and the killer of R. J. Weathers!

"Unfortunately, I don't," he said. "I mean, I remember the pitcher Steve Bedrosian, but I can't imagine why his beard has a website." He answered quickly and casually. "I guess they have everything on the Internet these days. Plus, it really was a pretty sweet beard." It didn't seem like he was lying. He *was* sweating, which maybe was a sign of a liar? But Mr. Bonzer always sweated. He could have been sitting on an iceberg in his underwear and he'd probably be mopping sweat from his brow. But I wasn't letting him off the hook.

"Bedrosian's Beard. Do you know it?" I asked again, pounding the table.

"Didn't I just say that I don't, Lenny?" he said. His eyebrows crinkled. It was sort of a guilty-looking face, but it might have just been that I was confusing him. "You're confusing me," he said. "Do you mind telling me what's going on?"

It was a good theory, the idea that Bonzer was PhilzFan1 and the killer of R. J. Weathers, but now it seemed to be a bad one. Nothing added up. But still, how was it possible that PhilzFan1 was posting from the library before it opened? I figured I'd just tell him the whole story.

"We've been following this guy on Bedrosian's Beard," I said. "He calls himself PhilzFan1. And he has been writing some crazy things. Some *really* crazy things. Things about R. J. Weathers. Who now is dead, if you haven't heard."

"I heard," Mr. Bonzer said. "I was watching the game. Such a tragedy."

"We were able to trace the messages back to here!" I said.

"Oh," he said again. "Well, I'm sorry. I can't

help you. Even if someone is saying something crazy on a library computer, we're bound to protect their privacy."

"Even if PhilzFan1 killed R. J. Weathers?" I asked. Oh yeah. I went there.

Bonzer stammered a bit. "Lenny, this is sounding serious. If you think that something like that is really happening, if this isn't just your imagination, then we need to call the police."

That pretty much made it clear to me that Bonzer wasn't PhilzFan1. Why would he want to call the police if he was guilty? But I hadn't revealed my final card. Classic move. I *was* a good detective.

"Some of the messages PhilzFan1 wrote," I whispered, "were sent *before* the library opened. I don't think it's a library user. I think it's . . . an employee." I cast my eyes around the room. No one else seemed to be working there, but you couldn't be sure. Bonzer's eyes lit up, a clear sign of recognition on his face. "Do you know the guy?" I asked.

"Yeah," he said, leaning close, answering my whisper with one of his own. "I do know the guy. Just about your size. Your age. Maybe a little taller. Nice smile. Brown eyes, brown hair. Wears it in a ponytail." He paused, and then: "She's spending the summer at my house."

I looked at the Mikes. They shrugged. Other Mike tapped his nose, which is something weird he does sometimes when he's thinking.

Mr. Bonzer pressed a button on his phone. "Maria, could you come out here, please?" A few seconds later, a girl who looked a little older than me joined us at the desk. Bonzer kept talking to me. "When the library's open, we pretty much have her working in the back, cleaning books, mending books, handling inventory, stuff like that," he said. "Mornings she's supposed to be doing computer stuff for the library. Oh, and where are my manners? Lenny Norbeck, this is Maria Bonzer, my niece. You might know her as PhilzFan1."

Maria's eyes got huge, and she started tugging at her ponytail. I thought she might make a run for it. "I—I, um," she said.

"I guess that's the end of letting you use the computers before we open," Mr. Bonzer said. "Lenny tells me you're in a bit of trouble. He's talking about the police."

"What—why?" she said. Her voice got all high-pitched, and she pounded the desk. Some library patrons looked at us. She lowered her voice. "All I did was write stuff on the Internet. I just love the Phils. Is that a crime?"

"No," I said. "I do not suppose it is."

So Mr. Bonzer was *not* PhilzFan1. Maria Bonzer *was* PhilzFan1. But probably not a killer. I looked at Mike, then at Other Mike. I could tell that they were thinking the same things. Where did that leave us? A killer was still out there. The game wasn't over. It was only the start of a new inning. And I was just getting warmed up.

CHAPTER TEN

The next few seconds went about like this:

"Dude!"

"Shhh."

"What the—?"

"Dude."

"Shhhh!"

"You mean she's—"

"SHHHHH!!"

"PhilzFan1 is Bonzer's—?"

"No way!"

"SHHHHHHHH!!!!"

A library is not exactly the best place to have a bombshell dropped on you. Hard to keep the volume down.

"Can we maybe discuss this outside?" I said to Maria, sensing the angry glares from the assembled readers.

"If it's okay with the boss," she said, pointing a thumb at Mr. Bonzer.

"What-*ever*," he said, sighing, saying it as two words, like a grumpy child. "I'd hate to take you away from your demanding schedule of posting incendiary comments on the Internet."

"Um, is that a yes?" she asked.

"Yes, that's a yes," he said. "Better than having you annoy everyone in here."

When we walked out of the library into the bright, hot sun, I swear to you, there was honest-to-goodness applause from the library patrons. They literally gave us a standing ovation, including the old folks for whom standing was a bit of a challenge. Even the gray-haired lady in a wheelchair struggled to her feet to show her approval at our departure. I guess we were making sort of a scene in there. Interrupting their reading and what have you. But never mind that! I had other things on my mind.

I sized up Maria. She was as Mr. Bonzer described: our age or a little older, with a slick bundle of brown hair snaking through the back of a red ball cap. As for the nice smile? You'd have to ask the Mikes. They were basically drooling at her

feet. Great. So it was up to me to begin the interrogation.

"Would you mind telling me exactly what is
going on here?" I asked. Seemed like a good way to
start. Her answered surprised me.

"Would *you* mind telling *me* exactly what is going on here?" she parroted. *Touché.*

"What do you mean?" I said.

"You come down here, acting all weird, demanding to know about stuff I wrote on the Internet, getting me in trouble with my uncle, who is
also my boss. What is up with that?"

"I—I, um . . . Guys, help me out?" I said. It was
all I could manage. She was furious! Her eyes were
burning, her ponytail was swinging wildly. Her
pointer finger was an inch from jabbing into my
chest. It looked like someone was going to get
hurt. And by "someone," I meant "me."

"Okay," Mike said. He was always good at staying calm. "I'm sorry we got you in trouble and stuff,
but Lenny was at the game where R. J. Weathers
died. He was supposed to announce an inning—"

Maria cut him off. "*You* were the one who won
Armchair Announcer?" she said, her voice taking
on a much friendlier tone. "No way! I totally

wanted to win that! Congratulations. That's really awesome. I would love to be there in the booth. Hanging out with Buck Foltz and Arnie Mickel and those dudes. Dream come true."

"Thanks!" I said. "Buck is pretty cool. Mick too. I was really psyched that I won. Only I didn't get to actually do any announcing. I think my dad was happy about that, though. He wants me to be a doctor."

"Well, yeah. What a bummer. I guess they had to cancel, under the circumstances."

"*Suspicious* circumstances!" Other Mike said.

"Oh, now I think I see where this is going. You guys didn't suspect *me* of having something to do with RJ's death, did you?"

"Well, um, I, sort of. We didn't know it was *you* exactly, and we sort of . . . maybe . . ." I was muttering, rambling, making a mess of my words. Mike jumped in.

"Yeah, we thought it was PhilzFan1, so, yeah, you. That stuff you wrote was threatening! What did you mean: 'a surprise in store'?" Mike said.

"I brought a sign to the game," she said. "That's all—TONIGHT'S FORECAST: BAD WEATHERS."

"Ha-ha. I saw that," I said. "Good one."

"But you said 'drastic action'!" Mike said. "I

mean, *PhilzFan1* said it, which is you, or whatever. I'm sorry. I'm having a hard time processing all this."

"Well, yeah, no," Maria said. "It *is* me, but it's not me."

"That clears that up," Other Mike said.

"Okay, dudes," Maria said. She was backing off a bit. Not quite so angry. "It's sort of like PhilzFan1 is part of me but isn't really me."

"Is this chick talking about multiple-personality disorder?" Other Mike muttered. He's not good at muttering. Maria heard him.

"I'm not crazy!" she yelled, in a tone of voice that made me not quite believe it. "I just . . . I just get so wrapped up in the games, and I just want the team to win so bad that sometimes I get a little crazy. 'Drastic action' didn't mean, like, killing a player or something. That's crazy. I was talking, like, a protest. A boycott. Burning all my team shirts, something like that. And believe me—for me, that would be drastic."

"You think *you* have a lot of Phillies shirts," Other Mike said. "If Lenny burned all his Phils shirts, the fire would be visible from space. You should see Lenny's closet. It looks like the Phillie Phanatic threw up in there."

Whatever that means.

Maria laughed. "So, yeah, well, I get carried away sometimes. A lot of times. Believe me. But it's just because I want the same thing as you guys. I only want the team to win."

"That's not all we want," I said quickly. "We also want to figure out who killed R. J. Weathers."

A light breeze rustled the trees. The bell from the Schwenkfelder Church tolled in the distance. A bunch of little birds chirped a high-pitched song while a goose honked bass notes in the sky. Somewhere a lonesome dog barked. Maria squinted at me and spoke slowly.

"And I want to help," she said. She spit into her hand and thrust it toward me. I didn't know what else to do, so I spit in mine. But I couldn't get a good spit because my mouth was feeling really dry. I tried, and a few sparse drips of spittle flew out. So then I just licked my palm. Both Mikes rolled their eyes and nearly fell over laughing. Maria kept her serious face on, so I did too.

"Put 'er there," I said. We shook hands firmly. I couldn't believe it. PhilzFan1 was going to help me find out how R. J. Weathers died.

CHAPTER ELEVEN

Standing out there in the hot sun spit-shaking and squinting like cowboys felt pretty good. Like we might really have a chance to solve this thing. But then a police car went screaming by, and the sound of the siren sort of popped my bubble. I thought of all the crime-stopping power in just one of those vehicles. Radios. Fingerprinting kits. Handcuffs. Weapons. We didn't have cars, we had bikes. We didn't have guns, we had our bare hands. We didn't even have mustaches. What kind of detectives could we be? Besides that, Maria was probably grounded. Mr. Bonzer certainly didn't look happy looming in the door of the library, shielding his eyes from the sun and staring out at us.

"You going to come back to work anytime today?" he shouted at her.

"I was hoping to take the rest of the day off," she said. "If that's okay."

"I'm going to have to have a talk with your mother about all this," he said. "You know that, right?"

"Come on, Uncle Alan," she said. We laughed. There's nothing inherently funny about being named Alan, of course, just that anytime you learn a grown-up's name you never knew before, it's hard not to laugh. If he wasn't just Mr. *Bonzer*, the library guy, but rather *Alan*, somebody's uncle . . . well, it makes a person seem more human somehow. "I'll mow the lawn for you," Maria said. This also made me laugh. Mainly because I was picturing Bonzer sweating all over a lawn mower.

"Okay," Bonzer said, sort of quickly. He probably hated mowing the lawn. He dabbed at his forehead with a handkerchief. "I'll let you take the day off to go do whatever business you're doing with these gentlemen." He pointed toward the three of us. We certainly looked like classy gentlemen. Other Mike was picking his nose (with both hands at once), and Mike was kicking the bike rack with the toe of his raggedy sneaker. I was actually behaving like a perfect gentleman. Maybe farting a *little*. "As long as you stay out of trouble," Bonzer said like he doubted it.

"You got it," we all said at once, Maria too.

"Great," he said, wiping sweat off his forehead again. "Cerberus has become Brahma."

"Um, what?" Maria asked.

"Cerberus is a three-headed monster, Brahma is a four-headed god. Instead of the three of you guys acting as one, now you're a four-headed beast. What dangers hath I wrought?" he said. Then he smiled. Librarians are sort of weird.

It was cool that Maria could have the day off with us, but I still wasn't sure where to begin. We stood in silent awkwardness in front of the library for a few moments. Luckily, Maria wasn't one to keep silent for long.

"Oh man, I can't believe you were there, in the booth, at the game when this went down, Lenny!" she said, turning to face me.

"Yup," I said, looking away. "I totally was." And then I didn't know what else to say.

"So did you notice anything unusual? Anything out of the ordinary?"

"He talked to the other announcers," Mike said, butting in. "And *they* reported observing a highly suspicious dork with dark hair and glasses farting in the booth. I think we should check into him. First name Benny or Penny. Last name Dork-back. Penny Dorkback, something like that? He's probably our man."

Other Mike coughed and they high-fived. They were hilarious. Penny Dorkback.

"Very funny, Mike," I said, blushing a little.

"Something shady definitely happened last night," Maria said. "Just think—what else did you see?"

"I—I—I really can't remember," I said. "It was all sort of a blur. I was so nervous and excited, it just— Hey! I was filming a bunch of stuff at the time. Maybe we can look at my video, see if we can find anything on there?" I sort of doubted that any key clues would be lurking on the video camera, but it was my best shot.

"Whoa, do you have a spy camera?" Maria asked.

"I wish!" I said. "It's just a regular little video camera."

"I have a spy camera," she said proudly. She put her hands on her hips and stuck out her lip. Very spylike. The Mikes looked impressed. She continued, "It looks just like a pen, but it does audio and video and everything."

"Is that the PCX05?" Other Mike asked.

"I don't know what model it is," Maria said, sounding annoyed. "It's a spy camera that looks like a pen, and it's awesome."

"Fair enough," I said, thinking that might come in handy later.

"So do you have that camera on you, or . . . ?" Maria asked.

"It's back at my house," I said. "I could go get it or whatever."

"Let's just go hang out there," Mike said. "It's hot out here, and I'm insanely tired of the library anyway." Then he added to Maria, "No offense."

"It's not like I own the library," she said. We stood and stared at each other awkwardly for a moment.

"Race you!" I said, rushing toward my bike and unlocking it as fast as I could. Then I looked back and saw Maria standing there with her hands on her hips, this time with her eyebrows pointed toward the sky. She whistled a little tune. "Oh," I said. "I'm sorry. You probably don't have a bike. It's not far. We could just walk or I could give you a ride, or whatever."

"Or," she said, pausing for a moment, then

grabbing the bike from my hands and jumping onto it in one amazingly fast motion, "I could give *you* a ride. Hop on!"

I stood there, blinking in disbelief.

And that's how I ended up riding on the handlebars of my own bike while Maria Bonzer pedaled me home. I was too mortified to speak. The Mikes led the way, turning around every so often to shout directions to Maria or to laugh at me. For some reason, I was wearing the helmet. Nice.

"Looking good, Snake Eyes," Other Mike yelled back at me.

"They call you Snake Eyes?" Maria asked.

"Snake Eyes . . . Killer . . . Nitro," I said. "You know. It varies. Other Mike likes to give us different biker nicknames. He likes to pretend we're a biker gang sometimes. You know. He's a dork!"

"I did notice the matching helmets," she said.

"Yeah."

"Hey," she yelled. "I want a biker nickname."

"Only if you can beat me!" Other Mike yelled.

"No fair!" she called back. "I've got cargo."

"Ha-ha," he said. "Lenny is cargo. Also you're a girl."

"Oh, it's on," she huffed, accelerating quickly. I

almost fell off the bike. My head was flung back like when you're on a roller coaster. I had to hold on for dear life, which was hard because Maria kept smacking me in the back of the head. She was really fast and, even with her "cargo," passed Other Mike easily. She held up her arms to celebrate.

"Don't let go of the handlebars!" I muttered. She paid no attention.

"Okay, okay," he said. "Your nickname is Armstrong."

"But I was using my legs," she said.

"Like Lance," I said. "Lance Armstrong—the bike-riding guy?"

"Oh yeah, him," she said. "I only know baseball."

CHAPTER TWELVE

That was one heck of a weird ride. But the embarrassment, it was just beginning. Somehow I had forgotten that Courtney would be at my house. Of course she was.

When we reached the Norbeck residence, there was Courtney, stretched out on the front lawn. She was wearing a blue bikini and sunning herself like a lizard on a rock. She looked at the four of us over the top of her large sunglasses as we teetered into the driveway. She didn't say anything, but she flashed us a smile I found highly annoying. Then she put her head back down onto the lawn chair.

I hustled the crew into the house. "Come on," I muttered.

"Who is that?" Maria said once we were inside. "Your sister?"

"More like his *sitter*!" Other Mike said.

"House sitter!" I shouted, blushing a little. "She's sitting the *house*, not me!" The central air was gloriously cool after the hot bike ride home, but I still felt like I was on fire. My face was burning.

"Ha-ha," Mike said.

"Shut up!" I said.

"She's really pretty," Maria said.

"I can't say I've noticed," I mumbled.

"Then you need to get your eyes checked," Maria said.

"My eyes are fine. I just don't like Courtney, okay? She's, like, four feet tall and a pain in my butt. How tan does a person need to be? Just . . . just stay down here. I'll go get my camera." I ran up to my room and started looking for my video camera.

"Is it okay if I grab a drink from the fridge? Okay, thanks, you're the best," Other Mike called after me while I was bounding up the steps. Idiot.

I ran back down the steps. I basically flew down. I don't know why, but the idea of Maria being in my house freaked me out. I wanted to get this over with. I brought the camera into the living room, where Maria was sitting on the couch.

The Mikes were pacing around, sweating, drinking orange juice, and looking kinda awkward.

"Here it is," I said. "Let's watch." The camera had a cord that hooked it up to the TV so we could view it on the big screen. I worked the controls and pressed Play with a sweaty thumb. Bad idea. Somehow the camera starting playing the wrong movie. Specifically, it was footage I had made of myself singing a rap song I sort of like called "Fistful of Dollars." And, yeah, maybe I was wearing some of my mom's gold necklaces and a pair of my dad's sunglasses because I thought it made me look cool.

"Uh, never mind that," I said. The guys were snickering *a little*. My face, it was burning. I pressed the button to jump to the next video, but it was another "Lenny alone" moment! This one was me attempting a dance move I had seen on a commercial. It did, shall we say, not go so well. You have to sort of run up a wall and freeze, but I kept just hitting the wall and falling over. The guys were at this point cracking up so bad that they had tears in their eyes. Maria was laughing pretty hard too. I thought they all might shoot orange juice out their noses.

"Shut up!" I said. "Stupid camera!"

Finally, I found the footage from last night.

Thankfully, there were no more embarrassing freak-outs. Man, I'm an idiot. The footage included some of the ride to the park. I was messing with the camera as we rolled in.

"Is that your dad?" Maria asked.

"Yeah," I said. "Who else would it be?"

"No, it's just . . . He's really bald," she said.

"Nice observation," I said.

I fast-forwarded through some boring footage of me walking into the game. It was funny—at the time I took the footage, it was, like, the greatest day in the world. Here's me parking near the VIP entrance, getting ready to be a star. Here's me walking into the VIP entrance, so psyched that I was going to have the chance to announce an inning. So strange how one moment everything can seem wonderful and the next moment tragedy strikes. Here's me walking past Don Guardo in the hallway. I kept fast-forwarding, looking for something important. A clue maybe.

"Dude, back up!" Maria said.

"We're not watching me rap again," I said.

"Thank heavens for that," Other Mike said.

"Fistful of dollars!" Mike yelled. "Hey, ho!" Then he got up and ran into the wall. Everyone laughed. My face burned again.

"No, not that," she said. "Was that Don Guardo?"

I had to admit, I was pretty impressed. She had done her homework. This was a real fan. She wasn't someone who knew only the good players— she knew *everybody*. She even knew the replacement catcher's *translator's* name. I thought we were the only fans that obsessive out there.

"I love that guy!" she said. "He gets serious fashion points." *Is she kidding? Do girls like guys who wore tacky suits and smoked cigars?*

"Yeah," I said. "I didn't get to talk to him or anything, though. I just walked past him in the hall. It was kinda cool to see him in person, but I didn't think it was a big deal or anything—"

"What was he saying?" she asked.

"Beats me," I said. "It was in Spanish. We took Spanish last year, but Señora Cohan was so boring! Pretty much the only words I learned are *rosbif* and *matemáticas*. Oh, and *panqueques*."

Maria gave me a quizzical look. "Roast beef, math, and pancakes?"

"Yup, you know, the big three," I said. "Kind of hard to imagine a situation where they'd come up, though . . ."

"You don't know anything else?" she asked. Then she sighed and tossed her hair. *"Qué lástima."*

"Hey, stop it. What does that mean? I just told you I don't speak Spanish. Do you speak Spanish?"

"Qué lástima," she continued. *"La persona que habla dos idiomas vale por dos."*

"Stop it!" I said again. "What does that mean? I know it doesn't have anything to do with roast beef, but that's about all."

She laughed. "Ha-ha. It means 'What a pity. The person who speaks two languages is doubly valued.'"

I didn't like feeling less than doubly valued. "I speak a little Yiddish," I said. "Like, um, *A chazer bleibt a chazer.*"

"What does that mean?" she asked.

"I don't know. Something about a pig."

"You're really great with languages, Lenny."

"Hey, guys," Other Mike said. "If Maria here knows Spanish, why don't we just play that part and see what Dom what's-his-face was saying? Maybe it's a clue or whatever."

"Don Guardo," Mike, Maria, and I said in unison.

"Okay, Cerberus," Other Mike muttered.

It wasn't a bad idea, though. He wasn't a great fan—he didn't even know Don Guardo's name or who he was. But maybe Other Mike was onto something. I rewound the footage (carefully) and started it up at the part where Don Guardo was talking. We couldn't hear very much of his conversation, and we had to turn the volume up really loud.

This is what the little man said, smiling into his phone, chomping on his unlit cigar: "O, sí, estoy tan ocupado. He-he-he. Mi hermano— Lo siento— Señor Famosa no me necesita para nada. ¡Estúpido!"

Maria's hand went to her mouth, like she was trying to hold a gasp in. She failed, and gasped really loudly.

"What?" the Mike-Lenny-Mike Cerberus said in unison.

"This is huge," she said. Then she repeated it. "Mi hermano— Lo siento— Señor Famosa no me necesita para nada. This is really huge."

"He said, 'This is really huge'?" Other Mike asked. "What's huge? He's little. Maybe he was talking about his cigar."

"No," she said. "He didn't say, 'This is really huge.' It's me saying 'This is really huge.' What he said that was huge is 'mi hermano.'"

"Hey," Other Mike said, hopping around. "I

know what *mano* means—that means 'hand.' So *hermano*, that's like . . . 'air hand'? Oh my God, this *is* huge! Don Guardo invented an air hand!"

We all squinted at Other Mike and cast him an epic side-eye. Maria raised one eyebrow. It was the appropriate response. Other Mike was out of his mind.

"Please don't tell me that Famosa killed Weathers," I said. I really couldn't handle the idea of my favorite catcher killing my favorite pitcher. "That will make my brain explode."

"No, it's bigger than that," she said.

"Bigger than my brain?" I joked.

"What isn't?" she said. "Zing!" She really said, *"Zing!"*

"Ha-ha," I said. "Very funny."

"I know," she said. "It was. Now, take a deep breath, because what I think you have accidentally uncovered here is a major scandal."

"I have?" I said. Then I added, "Oh yeah, sure, totally. All in a day's work for the great Lenmeister."

"Um, whatevs. But, yeah. What Don Guardo—probably a fake name—was saying was that Famosa doesn't really need him. Why would he say that? Clearly, because Famosa actually speaks English."

Now it was our turn to gasp.

"Why the front, then?" Mike asked. "Why go to all the trouble of having to travel with his dad to translate?"

Other Mike kept trying to reach over to the camera to rewind it, no doubt to replay the embarrassing moments from earlier. I kept having to slap his sweaty hand away. He giggled each time.

"Famosa probably just didn't want to have to talk to the media," Mike said. "Get out of doing interviews with those jerks like the Philly Hillbilly."

"No, that's not it," Maria said. "It's the other part. *Hermano.*" She pronounced it very carefully. Still, it did sort of sound like "air-mano," but I'm pretty sure air hands aren't, like, a thing.

"*Hermano,*" she said. "It means 'brother.'"

Cue the second gasp. This was getting pretty confusing. "Wait, Famosa pretended to be Don Guardo's son, but they're actually brothers? Why?" I asked.

"Okay, let's think about this," she said. "Famosa came from nowhere, right? Remember how the guys on the Bedrosian's Beard subpage about the minor leagues kept saying that he didn't have much of a history?"

"Um, no, Maria," Mike said. "Even we don't read the minor league subpages on BB. That's just,

like, a level of nerd I can't even begin to comprehend."

"Well, comprehend it, you turd bucket," Maria
spat. "Because it means something."

"What does it mean?" I asked.

"It means that Ramon Famosa is a fake identity. He could be anyone. He could be a Cuban
refugee. He could be anything!"

"Whoa, whoa, whoa, you guys," Other Mike
said. He had given up giggling and seemed to be
zoning out for a while there. Hardly listening.
Then he got really excited and hopped up, adjusting his shorts and smoothing his hair all at once.
"This is exactly like Warlock Mizlon escaping from
the Isle of Vor. In *Warlock Wallop Five*—the fifth
book in the greatest warlock series of all. I'm sure
you know what I'm talking about."

Everyone ignored this. But if you thought that
would stop Other Mike, you'd be sadly mistaken.
"Mizlon wanted to leave Vor because he fell in
love with a mermaid who was living in Taklin under the sea, but he couldn't leave because his father was the ruler of Vor, and if *he* knew Mizlon
was leaving Vor to be in Taklin, he would declare
war on the undersea city—war that would ulti-
mately destroy the mermaid Mizlon loved. He

couldn't risk having the citizens of Taklin keep his secret, so he had to sneak out of Vor and live in Taklin under an *assumed identity*. Of course, he then gets found out and delivers the famous 'for the honor of Mizlon' speech, but then there's a big fight and—wallop!" He slapped his hands together as if to say, "Well, that clears that up." Needless to say, it didn't really.

"So, um, sorry about that," Mike said. "You were saying? Why couldn't he just sneak out like all the other Cubans? Take a boat or whatever?"

I was thinking the same thing. I don't know a lot about Cuba, but I do know that there are some Cuban ballplayers in the major leagues.

"Who knows? Maybe he's afraid of the Castros," she said.

"Juan Castro, the infielder?" I asked.

"No," Maria said.

"Starlin Castro, the shortstop? Ramón Castro, the catcher?"

"No! Fidel Castro and his brother Raúl, you idiot!" she shouted.

"Sorry, I just like baseball. I don't really pay attention in history class." It's true.

"It's not history!" Maria said. "The Castros rule Cuba right now. They are dictators! Who knows how many great Cuban players we've missed out on seeing because of them."

It was silent for a moment. No one said anything. Mike tried to shake a final drop out of his glass, but it was clearly empty. I felt like I should say something, so I asked Maria if she was Cuban.

"No, I'm Dominican. Well, half Dominican anyway," she said.

"That explains why you speak Spanish. Doesn't explain why you're the niece of a white librarian, though," Mike said.

"Mr. Bonzer's brother married my mom. My mom is Dominican. It's not rocket science, duh."

"So you really think Famosa is a Cuban escapee?" I asked.

"I don't know. Maybe. And they're called *defectors*. *Escapee* makes him sound like a lion on the lam from the zoo," she said.

"Sorry. I'm really not racist!" I actually felt like I kept being racist by accident. It's a weird feeling. I'm totally not racist!

"I didn't say you were," she said, which made me feel a little better.

We all sat there in the big living room, with the white couches and the chilled air. It felt like a doctor's waiting room. No surprise, I guess. We were looking at the paused image on the screen. It was Don Guardo, grinning, looking sort of shady. Was he really Famosa's brother? And why was he traveling with Famosa? To keep a secret? To cover up a murder?

"There's one thing I don't understand," I said. "Wouldn't somebody notice such an awesome-hitting catcher leaving the Cuban league and showing up in the States?"

"Yes," she said. "I thought that too. But what I think is that they would *not* notice a not-catcher."

"Ah, I see. I mean, what? That makes no sense."

"Sure it does. Ever notice how Famosa kind of sucks as a catcher?"

We *had* sort of noticed.

"Yeah," I said.

"Well, here's what I'm thinking. They made him a catcher so he could be hidden. Maybe in Cuba he played another position so no one looked behind the plate."

"Or behind the mask," Mike said.

"Or behind the mustache," Other Mike said.

"Exactly!" I said. "I sort of knew anyone with a mustache like that probably had to be evil. I'm sorry—is that racist?"

"What?" Maria asked.

"To imply that a classic Mexican mustache is evil?"

"It's not a classic Mexican mustache, whatever that means. It's a ridiculous mustache. And he's Dominican, like me. Well, maybe . . . Anyway, the mustache rules."

"Finally, we agree on something. High five!" Maria did not meet my raised hand with her own. Totally left me hanging. Not cool. So not cool.

"It makes a lot of sense," I said. The pieces were slipping into place. "But how do we prove it?"

"And more importantly, *why* do we prove it?" Mike said. "Seriously, Leonard. Who cares if Famosa is Cuban or Dominican or from Mars? What could it possibly have to do with RJ's death?"

"All I know," Maria said, "is that if you're willing to lie and change your identity and fool everyone around you, you're no angel. And we're looking for a murder suspect, so I say we start with someone we know has something to hide already. Besides, if a pitcher drops dead, wouldn't you at least want to check out a shady catcher as a potential suspect?" There was a long pause.

"*A chazer bleibt a chazer*," I said.

"Um, what?" Maria asked.

"I remembered what that means," I said. "'A pig remains a pig.' Seemed appropriate."

"Yeah, whatever."

"So how could we possibly check up on this?" Mike said.

Maria shook her head like she pitied us. Like we were first graders about to take the mat against the high school wrestling team.

"What's that look for?" I asked.

"*Qué lástima*," she said again.

"Stop it with the Spanish!" Mike said. He cracked his neck like he always did when he was angry. Like a boxer, ready to punch.

"It means 'What a pity,'" I said. "She told us that earlier."

She looked impressed. "Maybe you *are* good at languages, Leonard."

"You don't have the right to call me Leonard," I said. "You have to earn Leonard-rights, kid."

She did not look impressed. "I'm just saying . . . you guys call yourselves real fans?"

"Of course we do!" Mike said. He cracked his knuckles this time. A little extreme, but she was getting annoying. "What do you mean?"

But before Maria could explain, Other Mike

interrupted. "Eh, not really," he said. "I don't actually call myself a baseball fan. I mainly like warlocks. *Warlock Wallop*—you know, classic stuff like that."

"Um, so you've said," Maria said. She seemed to be grinning just a tiny bit. Other Mike was winning her over. He always does. . . .

"Of course me and Len are huge fans," Mike said. "What are you talking about?!"

"You don't even know what's going on at the Franklin Mall this weekend?" she said. "*Qué lástima.*" Now she was just *trying* to make him angry. It worked.

He kicked the back of the couch and spat out, "There's a sale on bikinis? Why would we care what's going on at the mall?"

"You jerk," Maria said, crossing her arms. "Now I'm not going to tell you."

It was sort of crazy how well she fit into our group. I mean, yeah, she was making Mike angry and giving Other Mike grief, but that's why it seemed right.

"Come on, tell us!" we all said at once.

"Fine," she said. "There's a baseball card show at Franklin Mall *this week*. The Phils have a day off, and every year they have a player come to sign autographs. You'll never guess who is signing this year."

"I'm guessing it's not Pete Rose," I said.

"There's a baseball player named Pete *Rose?*" Other Mike said, laughing. "Ha-ha. Not a very tough-sounding name! An athlete named after a flower?!" He then started talking in a goofy high-pitched voice. "Oh, how do you do today, sir? My name is Pete Rose. And, hello, I'm Danny Daffodil."

"Not Rose," Maria said, not quite getting that I was joking. "It's none other than the famous one: Ramon Famosa." She paused for a moment. The Mikes paused too. Briefly, there was silence.

"Air hands," Other Mike said under his breath.

"Sweet," Mike said. "You think the Don will be there too?"

"I think so," Maria said. "I mean, he's gotta be. He's always with Famosa when Famosa is in public."

"Okay, so this is cool, but what do we do?" I asked. I mean, somebody had to ask. What are we going to do? Bring the video camera to Franklin Mall and show Don Guardo the tape?

"I say we bring the video camera to Franklin Mall and show Don Guardo the tape," Maria said.

"Just make sure you start it up at the right

point," Mike said. "If Famosa sees you singing 'Fist-ful of Dollars,' he'll probably die laughing."

"Then we'll have two dead Phils on our hands, Lenny," Maria said. "We do *not* need that." She high-fived Mike. Great. Now they were best friends, at *my* expense.

"This is all very funny," I said. "But how are we going to get over there? If you think I'm riding on my handlebars across the highway to Franklin Mall, you're out of your minds."

Just then I heard the *whoosh* of the refrigerator opening and the *clink* of ice in a glass. *Courtney.* "What's that?" she said. "You guys need a ride to Franklin Mall? I could probably take you."

"What the heck?" I muttered. Courtney never once offered to do anything for me all summer and now she's offering to take us to the mall?

"I needed to go anyway," she said. "There's a sale on bikinis."

The four-headed Lenny-Mike-Maria-Mike-Brahma-monster declared in one loud voice an emphatic "Ha!"

CHAPTER THIRTEEN

We had almost a week to wait until our big chance to confront Famosa at the mall. We spent the time wisely. I read a series of history books about the Crimean War and learned Portuguese. Mike mastered Bach on the piano. Other Mike trained for a triathlon. Just kidding. We spent it farting around on the computer and watching baseball.

Bedrosian's Beard had become less exciting since we now knew the real identity of PhilzFan1, but we still enjoyed checking in. There continued to be a lot of chatter about RJ's death, of course. It seemed like most people were coming to the conclusion that it was a freak accident. They were ready to get back to normal. The discussion returned to the usual stuff—balls and strikes, home runs and strikeouts. I wasn't so ready to move on. I was sure there was something fishy about the way RJ died, and I was sure I was going to find out what.

We were really excited about the chance to confront Famosa—*if that was his real name*—in person. Saying "If that is his real name" became a running joke with me and the Mikes. Any time someone said "Ramona Famosa," we immediately added "If that is his real name." We'd even started saying it at all sorts of other weird times. Once Mike made a comment about his mom, and Other Mike said, "*Mom. Pssh. If that is her real name.*" That's when we knew we needed to get out of the house.

Finally, it was time to head to the Franklin Mall. It was Friday. We had made plans with Maria so she could come too. Mr. Bonzer brought her to my house, which was a little weird. We were all farting around in my driveway when Bonzer's bright red car rounded the corner, tires squealing. He was a speed-demon librarian, I guess.

"Hey, Maria," we said in unison. Then we didn't know what else to say.

"Hey," she said. "Catch the game last night?"

"You know it," I said. It had been a good one. The Phils won, 10–2, over the Marlins. Their hot-hitting outfielder, Rafael Boyar, hit two home runs.

"Boyar looked pretty good," Mike said. He pronounced it "Boy-er," so of course Maria had to correct him.

"Boy-arr," she said, rolling the *r* in her mouth like the revving engine of Bonzer's car.

"Yeah, that's what I said."

"No, you said, 'Boyer.'" She said it in a very flat voice that actually did sort of sound like Mike. I giggled. Mike scowled. Maria continued, "He's Dominican. I know how to say his name."

"Wow," I said, trying to change the subject. "There are so many great Dominican ballplayers. Why is that?"

"Just something in the water, I guess," she said.

"Huh," I said. "I wonder what's in the water in Schwenkfelder, Pennsylvania."

"Dork juice, I'd guess."

"Hey!"

"Just kidding, just kidding. You dorks are okay."

"Thanks?"

Then Courtney came out from the house, dressed for the mall. It was slightly strange to see her doing anything other than tanning, but honestly, her shopping clothes were not all that different from a bikini.

"Shotgun!" Maria yelled, claiming the front

seat. This meant that me and the Mikes had to squeeze into the back of Courtney's tiny car. It was a Mazda or something, a bright blue vehicle hardly bigger than your little finger. Okay, maybe more like a midsized shopping cart. It fit Courtney, but squeezing in the back sucked, especially because somehow I got stuck in the middle and Courtney wasn't exactly a careful driver. She floored it around corners, giving the Mikes every opportunity to jab their elbows into my ribs. The music choice was pretty awful too, a loud, throbbing dance song where a lady or maybe a robot (or maybe a lady robot) was shouting. Sounded like something about fruit roll-ups and tube socks. Annoying.

"Can you put on WPP?" I asked, in between having my ribs pulverized by the Mikes.

"Ha-ha," Other Mike said. "Pee-pee."

"Shut up, Mike," I said. "It's the sports radio station."

"I know what it is," Courtney said.

"You listen to sports radio?" I asked, a little impressed.

"Sure," she said with a shrug. "Sometimes."

She turned the song off (thankfully) and let us listen to DJ Billy, the Philly Hillbilly. His loud, unfriendly voice filled the small car. He, for one, hadn't moved past wondering what had happened to R. J. Weathers. He was still fired up about it. I liked that.

"Something rotten happened on our ball field," he said. "This young pitcher was not killed by his own hand. He was not felled by the hand of fate. This was no accident, my friends. This was something far more sinister. Maybe the team doesn't want to admit it. Maybe Major League Baseball doesn't want to admit it. Maybe the city of Philadelphia doesn't want to admit it. Maybe the cops don't want to admit it. Maybe the whole world doesn't want to admit it. But this, sports fans, was murder. And, no, I don't normally buy into conspiracy theories. I don't believe that the government is controlling us through fluoride in our water. I don't think our digital TVs have tiny cameras so Big Brother can spy on us. I don't think that Connelly's Steaks' cheesesteaks are made from addictive substances—it's just that those steaks are so good! And I don't believe that an outraged fan from hundreds of feet away could have somehow killed R. J. Weathers. But I do believe that he was killed. And I believe, sports fans, that it was an inside job."

"Ew, can I turn this off?" Courtney said. "I like

sports radio sometimes, but this guy creeps me out. And I hate how he calls everyone 'sports fans.' That was such a stupid thing to say. And, like, a totally obvious advertisement for Connelly's. But man, it totally worked, because now I really want to stop at Connelly's on the way home."

"What's wrong with that, sports fan?" Mike said.

"Oh, don't you start," Courtney said.

"Sports fan," Other Mike said, laughing, elbowing me in the ribs.

"Yeah!" I said. "Don't turn it off. He might be creepy, but I like him. That speech gave me something."

"What?" Maria asked.

"A clue."

CHAPTER FOURTEEN

I admit it—me and the Mikes were making fun of Maria (and Courtney) for loving the mall, but Franklin Mall turned out to be sort of awesome. Okay, it totally ruled. There were a few malls closer, which is why I guess my parents never took me to Franklin. Also, Dad hates malls. "I have found that one's happiness is in inverse proportion to the amount of time one spends in shopping malls," he said. He's always saying stuff like that. He hates baseball and shopping malls? I suspect that he is not really American, possibly French, definitely weird.

Franklin Mall was really great, especially the food court. Me and the Mikes spent, like, an hour choosing what to buy but ended up just getting soft pretzels, which was what I knew I wanted all along anyway. Courtney left us, not surprisingly, to go shop for bikinis. We took our pretzels and went to get in line for Famosa's autograph. The line was pretty long, even though we were early and Famosa (*if that was his real name*) was, as I mentioned before, not a really great catcher. He was leading the league in passed balls and mustache wax and not much else.

Being in the line wasn't bad, though. I mean, normally I hate lines, but being surrounded by a bunch of Phillies/Famosa fans was nice. I felt at home there, you know? It was pleasant. Relaxing. Even though we were about to confront Famosa for being a fake and possibly a murderer. And that weird feeling of being watched that Other Mike kept talking about. But besides that: peaceful.

A very old man stood in front of us in line. He was dressed like he was going to church, with a tie and shiny shoes and everything. There was a red Phillies cap on his head, and when he turned around, I could see he looked happy. His face was a mass of wobbly wrinkles, but his eyes were bright and cheery and his mouth formed a crooked smile. He nodded toward the red caps we all wore (minus Other Mike, who just had a messy bird's nest on his head) and smiled.

"You kids big fans?" the oldster asked in a voice like a creaky door.

"Yes, sir!" Mike and I said in unison.

"Not really," Other Mike said. "Uh, sir." Then he whispered to us, "Why are we calling him 'sir'? Is he famous or something?"

"Not that I know of," I said. "He just looks like the kind of guy you call 'sir.'"

"I'm half deaf, but I can hear you," the man said. "You're really bad at whispering." He chuckled into his hand, then began to cough. "And, no, I'm not famous or nothing. Only if you could be famous for being a fan."

"You're a big fan?" I asked.

"Yes, sir," he said. I laughed. "My wife always accused me of loving the Phils more than her," he said.

"That's sort of messed up," Other Mike said.

"No," he said, drawing out the *o* like a song. "I suppose it's a fairly accurate assessment of the situation. Nothing against my wife, of course."

"Of course," I said. I didn't know what he meant.

"I've been a fan through some pretty lean years. There were some great years too, don't get me wrong. The nineteen fifty Whiz Kids. Bubba Church was injured, but we held on. Lost to the Yankees in the Series, though. I grew up when all we had was radio. There wasn't—and there *isn't*—anything on God's green earth nearly as beautiful as the soft *whoosh* you hear when you turn on the radio and know the crowd is there, cheering at the ballpark."

"Yeah," I said. I didn't know who Bubba Church was or what the guy was talking about really. "Are you a fan of Famosa?"

"He's okay. I have lots of autographs. I get one almost every year. Stan Lopata, Eddie Waitkus, Jim Konstanty. The vonderful Von Hayes."

Man, he was referencing some obscure Phils.

"You can go ahead of me, though, if you like," he said. "I'm retired. Got all day."

"Thanks, sir!" I said. "If you have time, may I suggest a pretzel."

"I think you better go before us," Mike said, breaking in.

"Why's that?"

"I have a feeling that after we're done, this whole thing might be done."

"What do you mean?"

"You'll see."

And I feared that he *would* see. I still had no idea how this was going to go down. We had to confront Famosa, and Don Guardo maybe, but in what way? We hadn't really solidified a plan. Maria seemed to know what she was doing, and she was the one carrying the video camera, but I wasn't so sure. There wasn't much more time to think about it, though, because the crowd broke into a roar. Famosa had arrived. He was escorted onto a little stage in the middle of the mall—I think it was where the Easter Bunny and Santa Claus sat. But without oversized eggs or reindeer. There was just Ramon Famosa (*if that was his real name*) and his father/brother—or whatever Don Guardo actually was. Bodyguard? Trained ninja assassin? Air hands inventor?

In person, Famosa did seem almost as unreal as Santa Claus. He had that huge, curly mustache, and he looked absolutely enormous. He must have been six and a half feet tall, and you could see his muscles ripple even though he was wearing a suit. He also looked sort of tired, with visible lines around his eyes.

"Man, he's huge," Other Mike said. "But we can take him." Gotta love Other Mike's confidence. Did he really think we were going to fight Famosa?

The line moved quickly, since most people didn't bother to try to talk to Famosa. It actually seemed like a pretty good deal, tricking everyone into believing you didn't speak their language. Most people would leave you alone. I decided I would try that the next time Dad asked me to mow the lawn. *"No speako the English,"* I'd say. Yeah. That'd fix his wagon.

Finally, it was our turn to get Famosa's autograph. And maybe a lot more. As we approached the stage, Maria rushed at Famosa. I quickly followed, the Mikes right behind me. Maria started speaking furiously, and I understood *"Hola, Señor Famosa,"* which she said with a polite smile, but that was it. Then it was just a quickly flowing river of words I could not understand for the life of me. Famosa (*if that was his real name*) didn't seem upset or anything. It didn't seem like she was blowing his cover and revealing him to be a murderer.

He just stared ahead, blinking and smiling. His mustache twitched. His eyes danced. He was either completely innocent or, in fact, a highly trained spy, totally resistant to the fierce questions flying at him. At least the questions sounded fierce. She could have been just complimenting his mustache for all I knew. Oh, how I wished I could understand what she was saying! Why did Señora Cohan have to be so boring?

Don Guardo *did* look sort of upset, though.

More than sort of upset. He looked furious. He chomped his unlit cigar and stared at Maria with burning eyes. He kept folding and unfolding his arms, then trying to shoo Maria away like she was an annoying little bug.

Finally, Maria finished her speech, concluding with the unlikely phrase *"¡Tango elf Konstanty!"* It might not have been exactly that. Maybe I was just thinking about the old pitcher Jim Konstanty because the elderly guy with the church shoes had been talking about him. Certainly the part about *"tango elf"* was probably just in my mind. No time for that! Things were getting exciting. Maria whipped out my video camera from her bag and held it under Famosa's sneering nose. She pressed the Play button with a dramatic gesture. Thankfully, it did *not* play the part of the video where I was rapping or dancing. But it did play the shaky footage I had recorded of Don Guardo, laughing into his cell phone about how he wasn't really busy.

Maria crossed her arms, satisfied, like she had solved the whole thing. Like she had just served up the final evidence on a silver platter. Famosa looked at her and shrugged. Then he responded. In English.

"Man, so what?" he said.

I suddenly became aware of all the other people in the mall, their voices buzzing like bees. And I definitely became aware of all the fans standing behind us in line, irritated that we were taking so long. The mall security guards looked ready to push Maria out of the way. Fortunately, they did not realize that one of the boys standing behind Maria Bonzer was a man of action. *Unfortunately,* that man was Other Mike.

Other Mike jumped up onto the stage in front of Ramon Famosa and launched into what he would later describe as "my own take on the famous 'for the honor of Mizlon' speech."

This is what Other Mike said, pacing around the stage like a professor giving a lecture: "We all know what's going on here, Mr. Ramon Famosa—*if that is your real name,* which I am sure it's not. You wanted to escape the sea—I mean, Cuba—but could not do so under your own name. You fell in love with a mermaid, and that mermaid was America. And to love a mermaid meant defying your father. It meant taking an *assumed* identity. It meant that you are really not Ramon Famosa, it means that you are the warlock known as Mizlon! I mean, um, that last part, I meant to say . . . You know what I mean." He shrugged.

Picture this: a thousand jaws dropping. A thousand heads being scratched. Three foreheads being slapped. But wait: it gets worse.

Famosa likely didn't understand a word of what Other Mike just said. I spoke English fluently, and this was not the first time I'd heard some blather about *Warlock Wallop* and even I hardly had any idea what Other Mike was talking about. I was beginning to think that we were totally wrong about our whole theory. Maybe Ramon Famosa was just a good hitter who sort of stunk at being a catcher. Maybe R. J. Weathers just happened to die and there wasn't any sense in trying to think it was anything bigger than that, much less that I could be the one to uncover the mystery.

Now Other Mike was reaching out like he was going to shake Famosa's hand. But he *wasn't* trying to shake his hand. He was trying to rip off his mustache. That's right.

Not being a mustachioed fellow myself, I cannot say precisely what it feels like when someone tugs on your lip hairs. Judging from Famosa's grimace, and the scream that followed, it's safe to assume that it hurts really bad. Among the painful things I *have* experienced are: brain freeze, paper cuts, getting my hand slammed in a car door, getting my hair pulled by Mike's sister, shots every time I go to the doctor, and the old soccer ball to the groin. I do think I have a fairly high tolerance for pain, but you would think that a major-league catcher would pretty much be top-of-the-charts in the category of ability to withstand pain. They basically make their living getting hit in the nads with baseballs. But, no, I never made such a caterwaul of pain as Ramon Famosa did when Other Mike tried to forcibly remove his mustache.

And, yes, sports fans, you have guessed correctly. The mustache was most certainly not a fake. After Famosa's strange howl of pain, it was Don Guardo's turn to yell. It was a deep, angry yell. Maybe a bellow. I'm not even going to try to guess what he said, but it was Spanish, and it was angry, and it was probably not PG-13. Probably not even PG-17. Probably nothing in the PG family. He hopped up and lunged at Maria. I thought he might punch her or choke her. Did he have a gun? A knife? But, no, Don was not assaulting Maria. He was stealing from her! He roughly grabbed my video camera out of her hands.

"Hey!" I yelled. "Give me that back." He did not listen. He put the camera under his arm like a football player taking a handoff. Then he started to run. He sprinted across the stage, then jumped off. He jostled past the crowd of confused onlookers and headed toward the food court.

"Get him!" I said. We jumped off the stage too, following him. I looked back to see what Famosa was doing, but I couldn't see him anywhere. Was he chasing too? Was he hiding? Maria sprinted after us—the five-person footrace was on. I just hoped Courtney remained occupied with the bikinis long enough that she wouldn't stick her head out of Bathing Suits 'R' Us or whatever and see us sprinting through the mall, trying to avoid mall security.

And, yes, mall security *was* chasing us. Two large men in bright yellow jackets were after us while we were chasing after Don. He was almost out of the mall. The long walkway reached the big department store at the end. What was he going to do, jump in the fountain? Sprint up the escalator? Either of those options would have been preferable. What he did instead was turn, bare his teeth—I swear he growled—and lunge right for us. We didn't know what to do, so we turned and ran! Now Don Guardo was chasing us!

"What is going on, Lenny?" Other Mike asked.

"I have no idea," I said, panting. "Nice work

with the Warlocks of Vor speech, though," I said between heaving breaths, the food court whizzing past us.

"It was . . . the . . . 'for . . . the . . . honor . . . of . . . Mizlon' speech," he wheezed.

"Got it."

"Hey, guys," Mike said. "Why are we running from him?"

"I don't know!" I said. And really I didn't. We looked back to see if Don Guardo was still chasing us, and sure enough he was. We were almost right back where we started, just a few yards in front of the stage, where we had just been waiting for an autograph. We were out of room. There were security guards to one side, Famosa to the other, the stage in front of us, and Don Guardo charging right for us like an angry bull.

Then he started to fly.

Technically it was more like a slow-motion fall, but it was sort of flight. He definitely was no longer on the ground but rather soaring through the air. Our old friend from the line had stuck out one of those old-man church shoes right into Don's path. (He definitely did this on purpose. It was awesome.) It tripped Don, and he lost control of the video camera. My precious little camera floated out of Don's hands as if in slow motion, like a baby bird taking flight for the first time. It was flying right toward Mike!

Mike looked at the camera, then at Don Guardo. The camera, then Don. Don was back on his feet and looking like he was about to tackle Mike. But in an amazing move, Mike reached up, caught the camera, and braced for impact with Don. The little man smashed into Mike with the force of a freight train, but Mike held on to the camera. Don bounced off and lay scowling on the floor. Other Mike, Maria, and I high-fived, actually pulling off the three-way five.

"You're out!" I yelled. Somebody had to say it. It really was amazing. Exactly like a play at home plate where the catcher takes a throw, holds on to the ball, and blocks the charging runner from scoring. A great cheer went up from the crowd. Everyone was watching. I don't think anyone knew what on earth was going on, but it had to have been a pretty amusing sight. People were cheering, clapping, and hooting. Okay, not everyone: the two yellow-jacketed security guards were not among the fans of this amazing play. They scowled and cracked their knuckles. They didn't know what was happening, either, of course, but they no doubt assumed we were in the wrong. We were kids. Kids running in the mall. Kids making grown-ups angry. Kids trying to rip off mustaches and annoying the celebrity guest. Were they going to take us to jail? Mall jail? Is that a thing? I suddenly looked around for Courtney, hoping now that she *was* watching. I was hoping that she could come save us, drive us home, and end this mess. I decided I needed to be nicer to her. She was just doing her job, just looking out for me.

But she was nowhere to be seen. Amazingly, the person who came to our rescue was Ramon Famosa. He stepped his giant frame between us and the menacing security guards and put up his hands.

"These kids," he said. "They are with me."

We were? The security guards looked confused—upset, even. They were probably really looking forward to roughing us up and kicking us out. Their fun was ruined.

Famosa, on the other hand, looked kind. I pretty much wanted to hug him. Especially after he said something to Don Guardo in Spanish that wiped the scowl off his face. Maybe he wasn't going to kill us after all.

"Is there a place we can talk?" he said to me. "Somewhere a little more private, perhaps?"

"More private than here? How is that even possible?" I said in a squeak, pointing to the huge crowd of people staring at us. It was a dumb joke, I guess.

Famosa laughed, then said, "Yes, perhaps somewhere a bit more private, such as possibly on the steps of city hall at rush hour or home plate in the middle of a game."

It was pretty amazing hearing Famosa speak English. He had a cool Spanish accent but was totally comfortable with English. He was completely fluent, like he'd been speaking it his whole life. Actually, he spoke English much better than lots of people I knew who *did* speak it their whole lives.

Just then Courtney pushed through the crowd, carrying an *enormous* shopping bag.

"What's going on here?" she asked.

"Man," I said. "How many bikinis does one person need?" Oops, I was supposed to be working on being nicer to her.

"Shut up, Lenny," she said. "I also bought a dress."

"Ha-ha," I said, even though it really wasn't funny.

"Miss, are you the one who is with these four?" Famosa asked.

"Yeah," Courtney said. "Unless they did something stupid, in which case I have no idea who they are."

"Gee, thanks," Maria said.

"Can someone tell me what *did* happen here?" Courtney asked.

"Perhaps we can go somewhere to talk," Famosa said. "Have you eaten?"

Maria elbowed me. Wait. Was Ramon Famosa (*or whatever his name was*) asking my house sitter out on a date? Things were getting really weird.

"Nope," she said. "You want cheesesteaks? I've been in the mood for Connelly's ever since I heard that stupid commercial. There's one right down the road."

"That is perfect," he said. "I shall meet you there."

"Did he really just say 'shall'?" Mike whispered to me, laughing.

"Yes," I said. "Yes, he did."

"Do murderers say 'shall'?" he asked.

"We'll find out," I said. "Yes, we shall."

CHAPTER FIFTEEN

We headed to Connelly's Steaks in Courtney's cramped Mazda. But I was in no mood for eating. I had questions. Lots of them.

My first question was for Maria. "What was it that you said to Don that got him so angry back at the mall?" I asked.

"*¡Tengo el justificante!*" she said. "It means 'I have the proof!'"

"Makes a lot more sense than '*Tango elf Konstanty,*'" I said. "But I don't get it. Proof of what? That he murdered RJ?"

"No, you idiot. Proof that Don Guardo is Ramon's brother, not his father. Proof that Ramon speaks English."

"What does it mean?" I asked.

"Well, we're going to find out, aren't we?" she said.

But what were we doing going to meet a guy who is possibly a murderer? I mean, sure I like cheesesteaks, but . . .

And would he even show up? We had just caused a scene in Franklin Mall and, by making him speak English, exposed him as . . . something. Even if he wasn't a murderer, which I hadn't ruled out, *something* was up. He definitely had secrets to hide. Why would he risk exposing them by being seen with us? He was a professional baseball player, which made him a celebrity in this town, even if he wasn't the best player on the team. He had to be furious at us. He had to want nothing more than to get back home or whatever and figure out how to smooth the whole weird scene over. The last thing he would want was to share a cheese-steak with the kids who'd unmasked his lie.

But, to my surprise, there he was. He had pulled his car—a totally sweet vintage black Mercedes—into the lot of Connelly's and was waiting for us. He leaned against the hood, smiling broadly in the bright sun under a large hat. Don Guardo stood next to him, a little disheveled and quite grumpy. Famosa's mustache was looking perfect again, al-ready smoothed and waxed to its ideal state. It made me laugh, imagining that he carried a tube of mustache wax in his pocket or maybe a whole box of emergency mustache repair supplies under the seat of his car.

Courtney somehow took up four parking spaces with her tiny car. We hopped quickly out—well, as quickly as possible with five people fighting to exit a tiny car at once. We crossed the parking lot and approached the Mercedes.

"Hello, my friends," Famosa said to us. Maria looked stunned, like she still couldn't quite believe this was happening. I couldn't believe it, either. He opened the door to Connelly's and held it for us as we walked in. "Whatever you want to order," he said. "Please. It is on me."

We ordered cheesesteaks the only way anyone really should be allowed to get cheesesteaks. That's "wiz wit." It means "Cheese Whiz" and "with" (or "wit'") onions. Anyone who orders them any other way is laughed out of town. My dad, needless to say, orders his with provolone cheese and tomato sauce. Blech. We also got large sodas, large fries, and, like, forty Tastykakes. Each. Hey, Famosa said whatever we wanted.

Connelly's Steaks was crowded, like always, and Famosa wanted to sit in the back, presumably so we could have some privacy. We picked the most secluded spot we could find and pushed two tables together so all seven of us could sit in a group.

Everyone began to eat. But even though I *was* starting to feel hungry and the food smelled really good, I had too many questions coming out of my mouth to fit any food in. (Even the greatest food on earth.)

"So is your name even Ramon Famosa, or was that a lie?" I said.

"Lenny!" Courtney said, scolding me.

"I'm just asking," I said. "You know, because of the whole . . . you know . . . thing?"

Famosa sighed, laughed, and rubbed his lip. "My mustache, it hurts." He scowled at Other Mike. "I wish I could get rid of it."

"It's a cool mustache, though!" Mike shouted, his mouth full of fries.

Famosa made the mustache do a little funny dance. He smiled. Even Don Guardo smiled slightly. We laughed. It was so weird sitting around eating cheesesteaks and joking with these guys!

"Ah, it is such a thrill to finally to be able to speak English! I have been pretending to not speak any English for many months now, which is harder than you may think!" It did seem hard, to have to constantly pretend that you didn't know what people were saying. And to have to pretend you needed an interpreter to do all your speaking for you.

"I was sure I was going to slip up sometime," he said. "But I kept it a secret for very long. Until *someone* let himself be videotaped explaining that even though he was here as an interpreter, he was not actually needed as an interpreter." He scowled at Don Guardo, who returned the favor. Famosa did not seem angry, though—just relieved. "And, no," he said, finally answering my question. "My real name is not Ramon Famosa. My real name is Jesús Marte."

"I knew it!" Maria said.

"You did?" he asked. He smiled.

"Well," she said, "I knew Famosa was a fake name."

"Very smart," he said. "Impressive that a young lady who is so pretty is also so smart. I can see why all the boys love you."

Cue massive blushing. Her, me, the Mikes, all of us. I think even the cheesesteak blushed.

After this long burst of blushing, there were more questions. "Was it true that you came to America under a fake name because you wanted to escape Cuba?" Other Mike asked. "Just like Mizlon was leaving Vor?"

"I am not sure what exactly you mean," he said. "But, no, I am not from Cuba. I did not lie for any reason but for baseball."

It sounded so cool how he said it. *For baseball.* We sat in silence for a moment, chewing, drinking, wiping our mouths with, like, a million napkins. (Connelly's food is good, but very messy.)

"Tell them the rest of the story," Don Guardo said. "Go ahead."

"I will," he said. "You will have to forgive my brother."

"We knew it!" I said.

"Yes," he said. "Don Guardo here is my brother, not my father. It was a trick. So I would seem much younger than I am."

We thought about that for a moment. "So this has nothing to do with Cuba or any secret escape?" Maria said.

"No, nothing at all. I am just a baseball player. All my life I dreamed of playing in the *ligas grandes,* the major leagues. But I got passed over by scouts again and again. I had the skills, but I was too nervous. Baseball is one of the only ways to make it out of the Dominican Republic if you are a poor kid. I wanted to support my family, to help my father. The pressure, it was too great. At practice, I would hit home run after home run. But at every tryout, I would strike out. Eventually, the scouts gave up on me. Then I gave up too. Until last year."

"What happened last year?" Courtney asked excitedly.

"My father," Famosa said. "He died." He made the sign of the cross and looked toward heaven. "And his dying wish was for me to make it to the *ligas grandes*. So I trained myself to become a catcher. I grew this ridiculous mustache. And I lied about my age. The scouts in the Dominican Republic, they are only interested in players who are basically boys. Once you get to my age, you are beyond old. But if I was young again, still a prospect—maybe they would give me a shot? All I wanted was one shot, to fulfill my father's dreams. To play one game in the *ligas grandes*. I was able to fake some documents, pull some strings. My brother here, he is very good at these types of things. He has always excelled in areas that are, how shall we say, not strictly legal. This is another reason why I wanted him with me. He is very useful to have around."

This made us a little nervous. Famosa or, um, what's-his-face continued.

"So now I have a question for you," he asked. "Why were you so determined to reveal my secret?"

I couldn't say it. I couldn't just blurt out that we thought he killed R. J. Weathers.

"We, um, we . . . well, I, you see . . ." I couldn't get the words out.

"We thought you killed R. J. Weathers," Maria said.

Thanks, Maria. Never one to dance around the point. What was he going to say to this? If it was true, we just ate cheesesteaks with a murderer. If it wasn't true, we just accused a guy who bought us cheesesteaks of murder.

Don Guardo laughed. Then he spoke. His English was also clear and perfect, though also tinged with a cool Spanish accent.

"I am sorry for my laughter," he said. "But the idea that Jesús killed that boy is laughable. My brother is the nicest man in the world. All that happened was that he fell in love with a mermaid, and that mermaid was baseball." He winked at Other Mike. Other Mike smiled a self-satisfied smile. "I was the one who told him to assume a fake identity. I was the one who helped arrange all this. And I feel so terrible that I was the one who blew his cover. Please forgive me, brother."

Then Famosa—I know Don called him by his real name, but I'm still going to call him Famosa, if that's okay, even though we have established that it is most assuredly *not* his real name—said, "It is fine, old friend. It is fine." There was a pause. "How about another soda?"

"Sure!" the Mikes said. I did not want another soda. I wanted answers.

"I don't get it," I said. "I have a question for you. Why are you being so nice to us?"

"Because I am a nice man," he said. "My father raised me to be a true gentleman."

"I see," Other Mike said.

"And also," Famosa said, "I need your help."

There was a pause then. A silence. No talking from our table. No talking from any tables. Just the sizzle of onions cooking and the quiet hum of the overhead fans.

"What can we do for you?" Maria asked in a quiet voice.

Famosa leaned in, bringing his massive head close to the center of the group. We all leaned in as well. It felt like we were in a football huddle or a meeting of infielders on the pitcher's mound. It felt like someone was going to tell us to try the hidden-ball trick.

"I need you," he said in a low, quiet voice that was at once friendly and completely terrifying, "to tell no one of my secret."

We sat silently for another moment. People chewed. Maria spoke.

"What will you do for us?" she said. Was she crazy? Okay, Famosa wasn't a killer, but he was still a huge man with a fake identity and a possibly insane bodyguard who'd just tried to steal my camera and tackle us in a food court.

"I am not sure you understand what I'm asking," Famosa said.

"Oh, I understand," Maria said. "You're asking us to keep this thing a secret. This thing that everyone in town would get a kick out of. Everyone in the country, probably. ESPN would love it. The local papers would eat it up. Bedrosian's Beard would basically go up in flames from all the shenanigans."

"Are you blackmailing us?" Don Guardo asked.

"Did you just say 'shenanigans'?" I asked.

"Blackmail, negotiation, call it whatever you want," Maria said.

"I call it shenani-*goats*," Other Mike said.

"Whatever. It doesn't bother me," she said. Man, she was tough. She was looking right at Famosa, jabbing a French fry toward him. "The point is, you want something from us, and we want something from you."

Famosa sighed and shifted back in his seat. "Fine," he said. "How much do you want?"

"Oh no," Maria said. "We don't want money."

We don't want money? Why was she saying *we*? There was no we in this blackmail. This was all her. But she continued, "What we want is your help."

"I am listening," he said.

"We want you to try to help us figure out who *did* kill R. J. Weathers."

"I am not sure I can do that," he said. "I am not even sure that he was killed."

"Well," she said. "We *are* sure. I can't tell you why. But we need you to help us figure it out. If it doesn't work, it doesn't work. But without your help, we are stuck."

"What do you need me to do?" he asked after a long sigh.

Without missing a beat, she rattled off the following demands: "One: we want you to leave tickets for us at the ballpark for the game next Monday night, with special instructions that we be allowed in the dugout. Five tickets under the name Norbeck. We'll be there early. Find us during batting practice. Two: we want you to do some spying on your teammates to see if anyone hated RJ or has any theories. We suspect it's an inside job." She took an angry bite of the French fry that she had been using as a pointer. Then she popped the whole thing in her mouth, folded her arms over her chest, and sat back.

"Do you promise to keep my secret?" he asked.

"You have my word, *amigo*," she said, and I knew she meant it.

"Me too, *amigo*," I said. The Mikes also said it. Maria stuck out her hand and Famosa shook it. Then he shook each of our hands. Then Don Guardo shook everyone's hands as well. It was a lot of handshaking, and I accidentally ended up shaking Mike's hand.

"Why are *we* shaking hands?" he asked.

"Just go with it," I said.

"You are a very impressive lady," Don Guardo said to Maria. "I am glad to be on your side. But as to you boys—" He pointed at us. All I was thinking was, *Please don't mention how all the boys love her.* "Why don't you guys just play baseball instead of running around playing cops and robbers?"

There was a moment of quiet, and then I spoke up. "I did play once," I said. "I was the worst there ever was. . . ." I let my voice fall off in that dramatic way. I always say that and always let my voice fall off in a dramatic way. I do this hoping that someone will ask me to tell the story. But, sadly, they never do.

"I was a pitcher," Mike said. "Until I blew out my arm. If I can't pitch, I don't want to play, really. I'm not good at any of the other positions."

Famosa smiled. "You should be a catcher, not a pitcher."

"Really?" Mike said.

"Hey, I saw the way you caught that camera and blocked the plate. You are better at blocking the plate than I am. You totally stopped that angry, angry base runner." He pointed to Don Guardo. Everyone laughed. Well, not everyone. Don did not laugh. He grimaced. He glowered.

"I totally did tag him out, didn't I?"

"Indeed, you did," Famosa said.

"I will get you next time," Don Guardo said. "I will be safe. *You* will be out." He was smiling, but he said it with a little more menace in his voice than I was comfortable with.

With that, lunch was pretty much over.

CHAPTER SIXTEEN

"Man, Maria, that was boss," Courtney said once we were in the car. (I was stuck in the back-middle again, for some reason.) "Really just extremely boss. I can't believe how you had them eating out of your hand!"

"Hey." She shrugged. "When you're good, you're good."

"Maybe you should have asked them for money, though," Courtney said. "He's gotta be rich! And he was totally ready to open his wallet."

I rolled my eyes and muttered, "How many bikinis does one person need?"

Maria laughed. "The great trouble with baseball today is that most of the players are in the game for the money. For me, that's not it. I'm in it for the love of it, the excitement of it, the thrill of it," she said. Everyone was quiet for a moment.

Courtney sped off, the car backfiring loudly, then lurching ahead.

"Um, that's Ty Cobb. I'm quoting Ty Cobb," Maria said.

She really was impressive. Who else had quotes from old baseball players memorized?

"You really want to solve this thing, don't you?" Mike said.

"Heck, yeah, I do," she said.

Someone blasted an angry honk at Courtney as she pulled wildly onto the main road. "Sorry!" She waved.

"You have fallen in love with a mermaid, and that mermaid is figuring out who killed R. J. Weathers," Other Mike said.

"That was really awesome how Famosa said I should be a catcher!" Mike said. "You really think I could do it? A big league catcher! Said I had good form blocking the plate!"

"Yeah, but he really sucks at catcher, though," I said. I don't know why I said it.

"Good enough to make the majors! And that's all I want. I mean, I think I'm going out for the team next year. Catcher. Famosa or Marte or whatever—he's in the bigs, and he said he thought I was great at blocking the plate."

"Technically, he said you're better than he is at blocking the plate. That doesn't actually mean you're great at it, because he's pretty terrible, but he is a big leaguer, so I guess it's sort of . . ."

"Lenny! Let me have my moment here."

"Sorry. Anyway, it's going to be awesome, getting into the dugout, looking for clues about the murder." I said. "So far all we've done is prove that Famosa is a liar."

"And you can't blame him, really. All he wanted was to play baseball. Nothing wrong with that," Mike said.

"Yeah, yeah, we get it," I said. "You're going out for the team again, Mike. You've made that clear." I can't explain why, but it made me angry. Okay, I do know why it made me angry. It was mean, but I sort of *liked* that Mike didn't play anymore. I liked having him sitting with me, putting our energies into cheering. Into being fans. If he got back out there on the field, where would that leave me? I know what you're thinking. I could go out for the team too. Maybe I already mentioned this a time or two before, but I *did* play once. And I was the worst there ever was. . . .

"I think that once we get into the dugout and

get some information from Jesús on the inside, we'll really figure this thing out," Maria said.

I wasn't so sure.

"We need Jesus and Jesús," Mike said. That joke makes more sense speaking it than reading it.

"I'm not so sure," I said. "I'm afraid we need one more thing."

"A clue?" she asked.

"No," I said. "A cardiologist."

CHAPTER SEVENTEEN

Courtney pulled into the driveway of my house, and I jumped out as fast as I could. I wasn't in a hurry or anything. I just wanted to get away from the Mikes, who had been sweating and farting the whole way home. Plus, I had to pee.

Courtney had her afternoon planned, of course. Trying on outfits and teasing her hair and tanning. Okay, I should really stop bad-mouthing Courtney because she had turned out to be sort of cool. Plus, she agreed to drive us into Philadelphia for the next Phils game.

Were we really going to be allowed into the dugout to look for clues? The whole thing was amazing. Millions of people had been watching Ramon Famosa all season. But only me, the Mikes, and Maria were able to solve the mystery.

Unfortunately, it wasn't the mystery we were trying to solve. It was like closing our eyes and taking a giant swing and connecting with a hundred-mile-an-hour fastball, smacking a massive drive . . . that ended up going foul. But it felt like we were getting closer to the truth. It was just a matter of timing the pitch right and soon enough we'd make contact. We'd figure this thing out.

Maria and the Mikes barged into the house after me. I hit the bathroom and came out to find the Mikes each on a couch. I took the recliner. It had been a rough day, but Maria wasn't about to let us relax.

"What did you mean before when you said we need a cardiologist, Lenny?" she asked.

"Well," I said. "We're still waiting to hear from my dad about what he's found out about the autopsy. We need to make sure it even *was* murder. It could have been an accident. Just a fluke thing. I mean, we were totally wrong about Famosa—"

She cut me off. "We weren't wrong about Famosa," she said defensively.

Other Mike started to say something, then stopped and went back to his paperback. Somehow he had pulled out one of those warlock books from somewhere and was already reading it. Did he stash warlock books around my house? Carry them in his pockets? Impressive.

"Don't even say it!" Maria said. She sure was good at cutting people off.

"Well, yeah, Famosa was lying and disguising his identity," I said. "But he had nothing to do with R. J. Weathers."

"I guess if you look deep enough, every family has secrets," she said.

I paused for a moment. "I don't think every family has secrets. Not mine. The Norbecks are superboring."

She smiled. "I believe that," she said.

"Yeah," Mike said. "Lenny's dad is a bit of a dork, yeah—"

"Shocking to hear," Maria said.

"But I don't think he has any secrets," I said.

"My dad was in a punk band in college," Other Mike said. "The Lactose Intolerants."

"My dad has a tattoo," Mike said. "Don't ask where."

"No, the Norbecks have no secrets at—" I started to say. Then I gulped.

"Why did you gulp?" Maria asked.

"No reason," I said, trying to play it off. "Just, you know, like a burp."

"That wasn't a burp. That was a gulp. I know the difference," she said.

"Oh yeah, do you?" I asked. "Is the difference between a gulp and a burp something you picked up at the police academy, since you're so obviously a trained detective, uncovering everyone's secrets and finding hidden locked boxes under beds?"

Maria turned her head slightly to the side and pursed her lips. "Who said anything about secret clues in locked boxes under a bed?"

I gulped again.

"Hate to say it, Lenny," Other Mike said from the couch. "But that was definitely a gulp, not a burp. You're hiding something. Time to come clean, gulper." He put the paperback down, and I knew this was serious.

Should I tell them that this summer had already presented another mystery to solve? I hadn't mentioned it to anyone, but I had been thinking a lot about the locked box I'd found under my parents' bed when I was hiding there the night RJ died.

"Okay, you guys, my dad has a locked box under the bed," I said. "I found it the night RJ died."

"Whoa!" Maria said.

"I'm sure it's nothing," I said.

"What do you think is in there? Secret cardiology things?" Other Mike said.

"Whatever that means," Mike said. "It's gotta be a clue."

"Only one way to find out," Maria said. She was already walking up toward my parents' bedroom. I didn't even know how she knew which room to look in. I guess parents' bedrooms are always pretty much located in the same place in every house. They always get the largest room, with maximum bathroom-closeness. It's not fair. I suspect some sort of a conspiracy.

"Dude, get back here!" I said. "I just said it's locked!"

"Good thing I'm a master safecracker," Mike said.

Maria came back into the living room. "You are?"

"Yeah, you are?" I asked. "Since when?"

"You're not the only one who's been reading books this summer, Len."

"I know. Other Mike talks about wizards constantly."

"Warlocks, Lenny. Warlocks," Other Mike said.

"So you're telling me that you got a book from

the library about how to crack safes?" Maria asked. "What kind of library is Uncle Alan running over there?"

"An awesome one," Mike said. "And, yeah, maybe I did read a book about locks. What kind of lock is it? A padlock? Chamber lock? Combination lock? Cruciform? Pin tumbler?"

"Dude, I have no idea. Cruciform? And how would I know what a pin tumbler is?"

"Try reading a book about something besides baseball," he said.

"Don't listen to him," Maria said. "I've been reading a Ty Cobb biography. It's pretty great."

"Shut up!" I said. "Would everyone just shut up? You know Dad'll come home if we go up there and start digging under the bed. He *never* comes home from work early. But it's pretty much a guarantee that Dr. Jeff Norbeck's shiny bald head will waltz right in early for the first time in the history of his life if we're in there. We'll totally be busted. I'll be totally grounded. I won't get to go to the ballpark to look for clues with Famosa—I won't get to do anything. So let's just forget it."

I knew it was a long shot. I knew they wouldn't forget it. You can't just gulp a few times about how you found a secret locked box under your parents' bed and hope that this crew would ever let you forget it. The odds that I could convince them to drop it and spend the rest of the day in a nice, re-laxed game of Hungry Hungry Hippos were next to impossible. Worse odds even than me *winning* said game of Hungry Hungry Hippos. I hate that game. I never win. Stupid hippos.

"You know I'm not going to drop it, right, Lenny?" Maria said. "I mean, that was a nice speech and all. But no offense—I wasn't afraid of Don Guardo and his pistol, and I'm not afraid of you."

"Wait. Don Guardo had a pistol?" I asked.

"Sure. What kind of bodyguard wouldn't?"

"Man, we could have been *shot* today?" I said.

"Not really," Maria said. "We were in a shop-ping mall."

I wasn't sure I followed her logic. But, still, I knew she was right. There was no way I was going to get her to give up searching my dad's locked box.

I sighed. "I think it's a combination, Mike," I said. "It felt just like the lock on the lockers at school. I didn't really get a good look at it. It was the middle of the night. It was very dark under there."

"You were under your parents' bed in the mid-dle of the night?" Maria asked.

"It's a long story."

"Dude, I break into people's lockers at school all the time. I could have done that even before reading *A Young Person's Guide to Safecracking*."

"I really am going to have to have a talk with Uncle Alan," Maria said.

We headed up to my parents' room. How could I resist? I really was worried about Dad coming in, so I asked Other Mike if he would mind acting as lookout.

Specifically, he said, "Just as the noble warlock Vander cherished his role atop the lookout tower above Katch, I will gladly serve as watchman. If a single intruder sets foot in our sacred land, I shall ring the magic bells and summon you at once."

"Um, just get us if you see my dad's car. Or my mom's."

"Got it," he said.

CHAPTER EIGHTEEN

Mike, Maria, and I made our way up to my parents' room. The house was empty—except for the noble warlock Vandey or whatever ridiculous thing Other Mike was calling himself—but we found ourselves sneaking. Very quietly we opened the door to my parents' bedroom, as if we didn't want to disturb a wild animal that might be sleeping inside.

Mom and Dad's room did not feel like a doctor's office waiting room. It was messy, filled with clothes and papers and junk. The door was always closed. The room was, in no uncertain terms, off limits. Mom acted like this was because she was "embarrassed about the mess," but was it really because of the secrets? One thing that was not a secret: she loved pillows. The bed was filled with more pillows than anyone could possibly ever need. Who could sleep on forty pillows?

The door creaked as it opened, and I felt my heartbeat speed up. What *was* in the locked box? Secrets? Lies? Guns? I needed to know.

I crawled under the bed. It smelled bad, as before. It was a little easier getting around under there when it wasn't nighttime, but it was still pretty dark. Also: the smell. Did I mention that? Because it smelled really bad. Maybe the locked box under dad's bed contained his collection of old sweat socks or hair balls coughed up by the neighborhood cats. It seriously stank.

I held my breath and scooted farther under the bed. I searched for the box, blindly groping until my hand hit metal. I couldn't exactly pick it up, so I just sort of shoved it. After a few solid shoves, the end of the box was peeking out from under the side of the bed.

"Land ahoy!" Mike yelled. Maria snickered. From under the bed I could hear them arguing about whether or not that was a dumb thing to say. I sort of had to agree with Maria. But it took me a while to inch myself out from under the bed, so I didn't get to participate in the conversation.

By the time I made it out, Mike and Maria were

quiet. They were in deep concentration as Mike held his ear to the box. It was a military shade of green and basically looked like a really big metal shoe box. A locked metal shoe box. Mike was examining the lock. He looked like a doctor checking for a heartbeat. Maybe *he* should be a doctor and I could enter his family snack-food business if the whole baseball announcer thing didn't work out. We could trade. Seemed like a solid plan.

Maria leaned in close, watching him work. I decided to do the same. I sat on the other side while he held his ear to the box and slowly spun the dial. At a snail's pace he moved the dial in one direction, then the other. After a few seconds, he declared, "I have no idea what I'm doing."

"What?" I said. "You said you break into the school lockers all the time!"

"Well, yeah," he said. "But usually I just grab them and pull them open. Those lockers are made of cheap metal and have been broken into about a thousand times. You just have to know how to pull. This thing has way tougher metal. This is one of those locks you can shoot with a gun and it won't open. You know those commercials?"

I said that yes, I was familiar with those commercials.

"This is totally one of those," he said.

"Got it," I said. "Well, I guess we're out of luck." I didn't really want to be doing this anyway, so it felt like a blessing. But, of course, the girl wonder would not give up so easily.

"Hey, Len, I think I know the answer to this. You don't have any brothers or sisters, do you?" Maria said.

"No," I said. "Where are you going with this?"

"Only child, eh? What's your birthday?" she asked, elbowing Mike out of the way and taking control of the lock.

"Why are you asking me this?" I asked.

"Shut up and tell me," she said. "It's not like it's a secret."

"His birthday is February second," Mike said.

"Groundhog Day?" she said. "Ha-ha. You're a groundhog."

"*You're* a groundhog!" I said. I hated when people told me I was a groundhog. It was a stupid birthday.

"What year?" she asked. Mike told her. She spun the numbers on the lock. Left, right, left. She took a deep breath, tugged on the metal, and smiled.

The box popped open with a satisfying click.

"How did you do that?" an amazed Mike asked.

"I never read the *Young Safecracker's Guide to Cracking Safes* or whatever," she said. "But I know that parents with only one kid are obsessed with them. Single-child syndrome. I'm the middle child of three, so I know these things. Lenny's dad's lock combination: Lenny's birthday. Easy."

"Aw, that's nice of Dad," I said. What? It was.

I shoved myself between the two of them to see what exactly was in the box. It seemed to be just papers. Lots of papers. Some in envelopes, some folded, some simply stuffed in there. Lots of papers. That's it. Nothing secretive and exciting. Just papers.

"Ugh, more reading," I said.

"Just keep looking through them," Maria said.

"What are we looking for?"

"We'll know it when we see it," she said. People always say that, but they never actually see anything. Or know it. They neither see it nor know it when they see it. Until now.

CHAPTER NINETEEN

Mike was the one who found something interesting first. "You guys," he said. He said it quietly, then louder. "You guys!" Then he said it a bunch of times like it was one long word. "Youguysyouguysyouguysyouguys!"

"What?" I said, annoyed. Then Mike shoved something in front of my face. It took a minute to process, and then it became very clear. Uniform. Mustache. Hat. Bat. Glove. This was a picture of a baseball player. This was a picture of Keith Hernandez, of the New York Mets. This was a very strange thing for my dad, who lived near Philadelphia and hated baseball, to have in his secret files. Even stranger was the fact that it was signed. My dad had met Major League Baseball player Keith Hernandez at some point?

Mike read the inscription out loud. "'To Jeff,

my biggest fan and fan club president. Always and forever . . .' Um, this part is a little hard to read. It's sort of blurry."

"I think it says 'Late to mass'?" Maria said.

"That doesn't make any sense," I said. "Let me see that. It clearly says 'That's so meat.'"

"'That's so meat'?" Mike said. "Totally. *Soooo* meat."

"Let me look again," I said.

"What it says," proclaimed the voice behind us, "is 'Let's Go, Mets.'"

Mike's and Maria's heads whipped toward the door. I didn't bother to look. I knew who was standing there, and I wanted to wait as long as I could before I had to face him. Dad. Stupid Other Mike. Worst lookout ever. The warlocks would have him fired or maybe chop off his head with an ax. Either seemed like a pretty good option to me. He was no doubt snoring it up on the couch, dead to the world.

"Oh hey, Dad," I said, still not looking at him.

"Do you mind telling me what the three of you are doing in here, digging through a locked box that was under my bed? Also, Other Mike, I like what you've done with your hair."

"Um, what?" Maria said.

"Just a little joke to cut the tension," Dad said.

"It's usually Len, Mike, and Other Mike. I don't recognize you."

"I'm Maria Bonzer," she said, sticking out her hand. "The librarian's niece."

"The librarian's niece," he said, like that made any sense. "Sure, sure. What are you and the boys doing?"

She blushed. It was pretty amazing. Maria had stared down Famosa and Don Guardo. She had bossed us around for days. She always seemed so confident and cocky, and now she was totally busted by my dad. Even though I was totally busted too, it weirdly made me sort of proud.

"Well, we, it has to do with, you see . . . we were . . . ? Um, Lenny, a little help here?"

I had no idea *what* to say. An unexpected Keith Hernandez situation can throw a guy for a loop.

"Okay, Dad, I know you're going to want to kill me for sneaking in here and looking at all your stuff, but I just happened to see this box and—"

"You just *happened* to be under my bed?" he said. I wasn't about to tell him the whole long story about me sneaking out, but thankfully he gave me an answer. "Aren't you too old for hide-and-seek?" he said. "We really should have sent you to summer school."

"We actually are learning lots at the library," Mike said. "For example, I've been reading *A Young Person's Guide to Safecracking*."

"I see," Dad said. "That explains a lot."

"Yeah, and I just sort of wanted to practice cracking safes. You know, my dad always says it's good to have a trade."

"I think he means more like plumbing, not breaking and entering."

"Ha-ha, yeah. Probably."

"I guess now it's my turn to explain a few things," Dad said. "I am pretty angry that you are going through what is clearly private stuff here, but we'll deal with your punishment later," he said.

Oh no! What if I ended up being grounded and missed my chance to go to the Phillies game to collect evidence with Famosa?

"Can we get to the more serious thing here?" Mike said. "The Mets?!"

Now, in case you don't know, let me tell you about the Phillies-Mets rivalry. Okay, maybe you're familiar with rivalries. Yankees–Red Sox, Army-Navy, Crips-Bloods (the gangs, I mean), North-South (in the Civil War, I mean). These things aren't anything like Phillies-Mets. We *hate* each other. People cheer when a player on the other team gets hurt. (Not me. I am a gentleman.) We have been fighting for years, and we certainly do not live in the same house as each other.

"Well, Mike, I do have a secret to tell. When I was a younger man, I was, in fact, on the Mets. I played center field."

"Really?!"

"No, you goof, I was just a fan, like you guys. A little obsessed. Okay, a lot obsessed. I tried to hide all that when we moved here."

"Why?" I asked. "I don't get it. Why would you have to hide being a baseball fan?"

"I'm not a baseball fan, Lenny. I'm a Mets fan."

These words were hard to take. It was like each word was punching me in the ear. "I'm" *ouch* "a" *ouch* "Mets" *ouch* "fan." I had no idea what to say.

"As you know, I am originally from New York. Queens. I loved the Mets. I grew up loving the Mets, what can I say? But then I went to college and medical school, and I ended up getting a good job here in the Philadelphia area. I made the mistake of mentioning my fondness for the Mets early on, and let's just say people didn't take it too well. Like, seriously not well. I learned quickly to hide it. I wouldn't have any patients! I was afraid I'd get fired! No girls would go out with me! A lot of bad things would happen to me around here if I admitted loving the Mets. You think a Phillies fan is going to let a Mets fan cut him open with a knife and mess with his heart?"

"Yeah, Mets fans don't know anything about having heart."

"That hurts, Lenny."

"Good," I said.

Then we heard a yawn. Other Mike was standing at the door. I think he was still half asleep. He was rubbing his eyes. "What did I miss, dudes?"

"Um, as you can maybe tell by the fact that Dr. Norbeck is in the room," Mike said, "you really suck as a guard."

"Also, Lenny's dad is a Mets fan," Maria said.

"The Mets!" Mike said it like the words tasted terrible.

"Um, what?" Other Mike said, yawning again. "Man, I *am* sleepy."

Worst guard ever.

Dad kept talking. I wanted him to stop, but he kept talking. "It's all just baseball. It all depends on wherever you were born. If you were born in New York, you'd be a Mets fan too. Or a Yankees fan."

"Bite your tongue!" I said.

"I know it feels like a big deal, son," he said. "I do. But it's just a team. Players get traded. The great Tug McGraw played for both the Phillies and the Mets. Plenty of players do. If we can cheer for a player who used to be evil, then why do the fans have to hate each other forever? Joe DiMaggio was a Yankee and his brother was a Red Sox."

"He was a Red Sox?" Other Mike said. "Wouldn't he be a Red Sock?"

"This is a good question," Dad said.

No it wasn't. They were both idiots.

"I think I need to be alone for a little while," I said.

"Um, I need to get back to the library," Maria said. "You're my ride."

"Wait. Did you also steal a car today, Lenny? Breaking and entering *and* grand theft auto? I think you're grounded."

"Bike, Dad," I said. "A ride on my bike."

"I can take you back," Mike said. "But I pedal. I'm not riding on the handlebars."

"Deal," she said. Then she turned to Dad and said, "Nice to meet you, Jeff. Go easy on Len. He's a good kid."

Dad just shook his head. I did the same. What else was there to do?

CHAPTER TWENTY

The next few days were a little strange. Me and the Mikes went to the library. We read some books. We watched some baseball. Okay, I guess those things don't really seem strange. But they *felt* strange. I was anxious and sort of nervous. I didn't really feel like talking to my dad, but I did want to know if he had any more inside information on RJ's death. The news reports and the Internet were quiet. If they mentioned it at all, it was only to say that there were no new developments. Dad said that his doctor friend hadn't learned of any new developments but that he still suspected foul play. I had to get to the bottom of it all!

One hot and humid day I decided to ditch the Mikes and head down to the library on my own. Just to get some new books. Maybe say hi to

Maria. When I got there, I asked Bonzer if she was in the back.

"Go ahead and say howdy, sport," he said, jerking his thumb toward the back.

I went into the cramped back office of the library. There was Maria. She looked really angry. She was supposed to be scrubbing dirty library books, but from the looks of the big messy pile in front of her, she hadn't gotten very far.

"You look ticked," I said. "Rough day at the office?"

"No."

"Getting worked up on the message boards again?" I asked. "Bedrosian's Beard?"

"No," she pouted. "I'm banned from there. So I've been listening to the radio a lot. I hate that Philly Hillbilly."

"What's he saying?" I asked.

"Oh, stupid stuff. About how the fans need to be *tougher* on the team. Doesn't he remember that someone just killed a guy? Does he want it to happen again? Someone needs to stop him."

"Yeah, he's a jerk," I said. "But he's harmless. My dad says it's just shtick."

"What does that mean?" she asked.

"Just, like, it's all an act. He only says outland-
ish things to get ratings."

"I like that. Shtick. I like your dad," she said.
She smiled and halfheartedly wiped at a dirty
book. I don't mean a *dirty* book. Just that someone
spilled soda on it or whatever.

"He's a Mets fan!" I said.

"But he's funny. Shtick."

"Trust me. He really isn't."

Maria hummed a few bars of some song I
couldn't place, then went back to wiping books.

"Maybe there's more to him than we think,"
she said.

"My dad? I thought we established his deep,
dark secret."

"No, Lenny—Billy, the radio guy."

"I don't think so," I said. "You think he had
something to do with RJ?"

"Maybe. Wasn't he there at the game?"

"I guess so. I didn't see him. There were fifty
thousand people there, though. They can't all be
suspects."

"I'd say we have forty-nine thousand nine hundred and ninety-nine suspects, and I'm not resting
until we're down to just one," she said.

"Only forty-nine thousand nine hundred and ninety-nine?" I said. "Counting me out? Thanks."

"I was counting your dad out. I still haven't made my mind up about you."

"Thanks," I said.

She glared at me over the stack of books. "I still think we need to ask DJ Billy Philly Hillbilly some questions," she said. "Something tells me he knows more than he's saying. Let's talk to him. For questioning."

"I tried to get through once before. It was just busy," I said. "There must be a million people calling."

"They'll always answer if a pretty girl calls," she said, batting her eyelashes.

"Well, where are we going to get one of those?" I said, just teasing.

Oh, my friends, if looks could kill, as they say. It doesn't even begin to describe it. This look didn't just kill, it annihilated and ate the bones.

"Hand me the phone, jerk."

I grabbed the old, yellowed library phone and tossed it to her. The cord made it snap back, knocking over a pile of books. "Um, I forgot it had a cord," I said. Good one, Len.

"Uncle Alan, I'm making a personal call that could probably take a while," she said.

"Employee of the year!" I heard him say from the other room.

She dialed the number. It rang for a little while. When the person on the other end answered, she started talking in a voice I could hardly recognize. She made her accent a little heavy and sounded quite a bit like a movie star!

"Hello there," she said.

"Is that him?" I asked excitedly.

"I would like very much to talk to Billy, please," she said into the phone. Oh, probably not. "My question?" She sounded annoyed. "Listen, sweetheart, I do not have time for these sorts of games. Just put me through to him." Did she really just call someone "sweetheart"?

They must have put her on hold because she started impatiently twirling the phone cord. "Yeah, hello?" she said after a few minutes. She was on the air! She dropped the soft, movie star voice and started barking like her old self. "This is Maria from Schwenkfelder. Shut up! Yes, that's a real place. Stop asking me questions! I have questions for you." I could imagine the other half of this conversation. His obnoxious comebacks. His dumb sound effects. (Okay, some of those sound effects are pretty great. *Plbbbbt!*) She grilled him right back. She barely let him get a word in! She demanded that he stop riling up the fans and demanded that he tell her what he knew about RJ. Eventually, he must have hung up. "You're a jerk!" she yelled, over and over again. "You're a jerk! You're a jerk!" Then she slammed down the phone.

"I guess he was being a jerk," I said.

She did not smile. "He really is," she said. "But I'm just wasting time here. Who am I fooling? He had nothing to do with RJ. I'm sure of it. Oh, why are we stuck here?"

So that was that.

"Sooo," I said, not sure what else to say. "Excited about the game on Monday?"

"You know it. We gotta find a clue. Plus, you know, I just love baseball." She smiled weakly and spun the phone cord.

"Me too," I said. "Me too."

There was another pause. "Hey, that reminds me. I wanted to ask you: why don't you play ball if you're so into it?"

Oh, Jesús Marte, I did *not* like it when people

asked me this question. I tried to give my standard answer. "I did play once. I was the worst there ever was. . . ."

"You keep saying that. What does that mean? You still play or what?"

"Well, I used to play, but I, um, I got cut."

"Cut from the team?"

"No, cut with a knife."

"Ooh, sounds dramatic!"

"Actually, I quit. I thought that was obvious."

"Well, it wasn't. Anyway, now you *have* to tell me."

She said I had to. I didn't want to, but it was time. So now, my friends, it is time for me to finally regale you with the story of my baseball career. About how I was the worst player ever.

My career officially ended two years ago. And I'm not proud of the reasons behind it, but in the interest of honesty, I guess now is the time to share.

The pitcher was a huge fifth grader—a giant kid who made me think that Little League should start its own policy on steroid testing. This pitcher was an absolute monster—like, the C. C. Sabathia of Little League. With a curveball like Tim Lincecum. A fastball like Randy Johnson in his prime. A nasty snarl like the best big league closers. Oh, and a couple of cute blond pigtails. Her name was Kimberly Watson.

There was a girls softball team, but Miss Watson wanted to play hardball, and they let her. They thought her parents would sue or whatever if they refused. But no one thought about my safety! And sanity!

Do you know how it feels to be reduced to tears by a smoke-throwing girl? Truth is, I wasn't the only guy to shed a tear after being whiffed by Watson. We even had a little club called "Whiffed by Watson." It was ironic, I guess, and we usually laughed about it. But inside we weren't laughing. She threw so hard! And sometimes she was wild. Once a guy named Spencer Perk thought he got a hit because he closed his eyes and swung, then heard a bong and opened his eyes. The ball was near third base so he started running. But really it was a wild pitch—the ball had rebounded off the bars on top of the batting cage and bounced all the way back in play! He missed making contact by literally twenty feet but thought he got a hit. When he realized what had happened—and why everyone was laughing—he was pretty embarrassed. He had to walk back from first to the batter's box.

It was an embarrassing thing for Spencer Perk, but I was in a class all my own. I wasn't the only one whose career was ended by Miss Watson, but I had the most epic "Whiffed by Watson" tale of all. It was toward the end of a one-sided loss. We were behind, something like 6–0. A six-run deficit against Kimberly Watson was like being behind 100–0 against most pitchers, with two strikes and two outs in the bottom of the last at bat. Even still, I only got my one at bat and two innings in lonely right field. And of course when I came to bat against Watson, with nobody on and two outs in the last inning, everyone started heading home. Even my dad had his keys out. He was probably trying to beat traffic. No one had any hopes that I would start a rally.

No one had any hopes that I would reach base. No one had any hopes that I would even manage a meager foul tip. But there are actually more than twenty different ways to reach first base. And number three on the list doesn't require anything much from the batter. You don't have to have the patience to work four balls. You don't have to have a solid stroke to get a hit. You just have to stand there. Which is exactly what I did. I was terrified to be up there against Kimberly Watson. I didn't want to end the game. I didn't want to get whiffed by a girl. I decided that I wouldn't swing. She could just groove three strikes down the middle and I could go home with whatever small dignity I could muster. "Come on now, Lenny!" I heard from the crowd as the first pitch zoomed right down the heart of the plate. It smacked the catcher's mitt with a noise like a rifle shot.

"Take a cut!" my coach yelled. No, I decided. I would not. I would not take a cut. And somehow I guess this offended Kimberly Watson.

"Take a swing at this next one or pitch number three is in your ear!" she yelled. I heard laughter from the bleachers. This was funny? How was it not illegal? How was it okay to threaten a kid with a fastball to the ear? If a guy did it, they'd throw him out of the game for sure. But a girl? Somehow all bets were off. I called time.

"You hear that, ump?" I asked. "She said she's gonna hit me." My heart was beating in my throat. I guess I said it pretty loud because she heard me from the pitcher's mound.

"I'm not really gonna hit you!" she shouted back. "I ain't gonna hit him, ump," she said.

"Shut up and take a swing," the ump said. But I did not. I let pitch two zoom over the plate for a second strike. Watson smiled. I grimaced. Of course she would tell the ump that she wasn't going to hit me, but I didn't believe her. That smile. So evil. I knew. I just knew she was going to put a hundred-mile-an-hour fastball in my ear. And I really did not like the idea of having to go to the emergency room with a Rawlings lodged in my ear canal. And what I liked least of all was the idea of having to explain to the doctor that the baseball got lodged in my ear by a girl.

She stared at me with those evil eyes. She licked her evil lips. I heard the umpire giggle. I tried to call time-out again.

"Get in there, kid," he said. "I don't want to crouch back here all day. My knees are killing me." I tapped the plate with my bat. Tap, tap. I tapped my cleats with my bat. Tap, tap. I put the bat on my shoulder. Miss Watson reared back in that slow and crazy windup she has, and I closed my eyes. I saw the ball fly from her hand, and I hit the dirt. I mean, I dropped to the ground faster than the Cubs drop from the play-offs every year. I was so sure that the ball was going to hit me in the head that I actually felt a burn in my ear. And then I heard the ump scream, "Strike three!"

It was a perfect strike. An eephus pitch. That's

like a soft lob. Slower than a changeup—the slowest pitch of all. An extremely slow, soft toss, nothing more than an arcing lob a baby could catch with a bare hand. An eephus. Right into the catcher's mitt. But I didn't know that yet. My eyes were squeezed shut. I was curled into a ball in the dirt. And all I could feel was wetness down my leg. Yes, sports fans, a girl pitcher made me pee my pants.

It was then—yes—exactly then, that I decided to become an announcer. It was hard to imagine any scenario that ended in an announcer whizzing himself. Maybe an extra-inning game where you had too many sodas? Well, that's probably why announcers always work in teams. In case someone needs to pee. Yeah, behind the microphone, behind the glass, in the booth. That was the place for me. This I knew, lying there pee-soaked in the dirt, hearing the roaring laughter of the crowd and the *thwack* of high fives as Kimberly Watson's teammates smacked her victorious palm. Yeah.

The Mikes knew about this event. Everyone at school knew about it. This was the type of thing that spreads faster than poison ivy at summer camp. But—and this is why they are the best friends in the history of the world—neither one of them ever mentioned it. Not once. I was the worst there ever was, and it was very humiliating.

I told that to Maria, just, you know, in a slightly shortened version. I left out some of the details. I'm sure you can forgive me. Basically, she just shrugged.

"You're not the worst in my book," she said, pausing as if about to say more.

"I'm the best?" I offered hopefully.

"Don't push it, dork," she said. "Don't push it."

CHAPTER TWENTY-ONE

The next red-letter day of the summer had arrived. Plans were made. Dad would drive. I think Courtney was a little bummed that she wouldn't get to come to the game. But, no, sadly, she wouldn't be using that fifth ticket. Who would? Jeff Norbeck, of course. After all, it *was* a Mets game. He even took off from work early so we could get there early. After all, *we* had work to do.

I was pacing around, waiting for him to come down from his room. He had rushed in and said he was going to get changed before we left to pick Maria and the Mikes up. I spent the time pretending to bunt for base hits with an imaginary bat and ball in the living room. Finally, he strolled downstairs, smiling.

"You are *not* going to wear that!" I said. He was

dressed head to toe in Mets gear. He was the Mets mascot, Mr. Met, come to life. I wanted to barf.

"I most certainly *am* going to wear this," he said. "Is the button too much?"

"Which one?" I asked. He had about fifty Mets buttons on. "Please, Dad. Take that stuff off. I'd like to live to see my teenage years," I said. "Find out what all the fuss is about."

"Oh, don't overreact, Len," he said, looking at himself in the mirror above the couch, grinning like a monkey.

"People do get killed for wearing the wrong hat," I said. "Or at least beat up. It happens all the time. I am not joking."

"No one will beat up a harmless cardiologist out for an evening ball game with his son and his friends," he said. "This is America. We're all going to be there because we love baseball!" He sang it like a Broadway show tune. All these years of holding in his baseball fandom was making him strange. It was pouring out, like a garden hose finally un-kinked.

"I'm sorry," I said. "Are you new to Philadel-phia? You might get eaten alive. Literally." He laughed. He really thought it was funny! "What happened to worrying about your job?" I asked. "What happened to caring about your reputation? What happened to worrying about making sure you had patients?"

"Ah, I've been at that hospital forever by now. No one could take my job if they wanted to. I have more patients than I know what to do with."

"Philly is a good town for heart attacks, I guess. Probably all the lousy sports teams and cheese-steaks."

"You said it, kid!"

"Hey, can we go?" It was still early, and the game was a late start due to it being the nationally televised game of the week. It started at eight. Actually, eight-oh-five. Ever notice how baseball games never start exactly on the hour? It's always like seven-oh-five or one-thirty-five or something weird. I suspect some sort of conspiracy.

We made our rounds and Dad was even cool about all the extra driving he had to do. Wearing that stupid Mets getup really put him in a good mood, I guess. I wasn't in precisely such an excellent mood myself. Were we even going to have tickets? Was Famosa going to follow through with his promise for VIP tickets? (Man, I could really get used to all this very-important-Lenny stuff.)

What if Famosa forgot? Or chose to ignore us? We were just a bunch of kids. But, no, we weren't! We had the power to share his secret with the world. Bedrosian's Beard had even been buzzing a bit about the scene at Franklin Mall. We were famous! Sort of. There were lots of rumors and inaccurate stories about what went down with Famosa. No one was close to guessing the truth, which was probably too unbelievable to accept. People mostly just thought that some insane kids off their meds jumped the line and caused a scene. No one deduced that it was a few kids investigating a crime who tried to pull off Famosa's mustache and ended up figuring out his fake identity.

But the truth of what went down in that mall hadn't hit the media. I suspected that Don Guardo was good at his job. Maybe he was a fake interpreter, but he was very good at guarding Famosa—and his secrets. I didn't know what magic he'd pulled to keep the story off TV and mostly hush-hush, but I was sure he did something.

Dad turned on the radio and tuned in WPP without even being asked. "I know you kids like this sports radio guy," he said. "So I'll put him on for you."

"Meh. We don't love the Philly Hillbilly

anymore," Maria said. She was slumped low in the seat in the back. "He was mean to me."

"Well, all right!" Dad said. "I hope you will accept a high five from a Mets fan. I mean, an imaginary high five because I do not want to take my hands off the wheel in this traffic."

We laughed. What a dork.

The traffic really was bad as we drove away from the Schwenkfelder quiet into the city. Everyone seemed to be honking at once. We were moving at a slow crawl. I leaned back into my leather seat and nervously drummed my fingers on the armrest. Slowly, the city rose before us in the distance. Skyscrapers loomed. Soon we'd see the ballpark.

My mind went back to the last time I was here. The night RJ died. The night RJ was *killed*. Was I returning this night to solve the murder? A theory had already started to loosely come together in my mind. Was I right? Was I going to be able to find proof? Or was another twist coming my way?

We arrived at the park. It was about six o'clock. The sun still sat high on its perch, waiting patiently for its cue to descend. It was a warm evening, but not sweaty. The world felt like a loaf of freshly baked bread. It was beautiful. Dad parked the car and we weren't outside in the parking lot for more than two seconds when we heard "Mets suck!" for the first time. We would hear it many more times. I thought I might die of embarrassment.

Dad didn't mind. He smiled. "I feel like a man liberated from a life of lies," he said. He really honestly says stuff like that all the time.

"How can people get so worked up about a hat?" Other Mike said. I tried to think up a warlock-related description that would work here but couldn't. Mainly I wanted to slap him.

"Dad, do you have to be the most embarrassing dad in the history of dads?" I asked.

"Yes," he sang. "Yes, I do!" Then he started a chant of "Let's go, Mets!" that I was sure was going to get us killed. Most people took it pretty well, actually. There was some teasing and so forth, but I didn't feel like I was going to be murdered. I suspected that might change by around the fifth inning, but so far, so good.

"Dad, you are going to have to stay out of the dugout, though," I said. "You know that, right? You cannot go into the Phils dugout wearing that hat."

"I don't want to anyway," he said. "I'll stay in

our seats to watch batting practice. You go gather clues. Make me proud."

As we walked toward the ticket window, a guy played the *Rocky* theme song on a saxophone. He probably did that before every game, hoping people would throw quarters in his case. But I felt like it was just for me. And I felt inspired.

We walked up to the ticket booth and got in line. A few fans yelled at Dad. He ignored them. Finally, it was our turn. "There should be some tickets here for Norbeck," Dad said to the lady behind the counter. And sure enough there were. We each got a ticket and a bright yellow VISITOR tag to wear around our necks. Famosa had come through for us! We took the tickets and walked into the park. I got that tight feeling in my chest I always get when I enter the ballpark. It's my favorite place on earth.

"I guess these visitor passes let us into the dugout?" I said.

"Even the murderous PhilzFan1?" Mike said, teasing Maria.

"I don't know," she said with a laugh. "He still might be out there, lurking among us. Ready to bite the heads off the team if they fail."

We walked farther into the ballpark. It was

such a great feeling to be in a sea of fans, all dressed in red. (Except for, you know, a few weirdos and/or cardiologists.) The game was a while away, but the energy of the ballpark before game time was unmistakable. Plus, we had our own plans for the night. Or did we?

"What's the plan?" I said to Maria.

"Well," she said, "I'm thinking we should get Famosa's attention and he'll take us into the dugout to look for clues."

"I don't know if security is *that* relaxed," I said.

Those yellow visitor passes were pretty amazing. No one stopped us no matter where we walked in the park. Maria led us down the aisle right up to the dugout where the Phils players were getting ready. She started yelling "Jesús!" then she covered her mouth with her hand. "Oops!" She corrected herself and said, "Ramon! Señor Famosa!"

She yelled this a few dozen times. She really does have a loud voice. And sure enough, Famosa popped up. He looked like a turtle emerging from his shell as he stuck his head out of the dugout. *"Hola, amiga,"* he said. Even I knew what that meant. Then they started talking back and forth really quickly, a river of Spanish words I couldn't hope to understand. He smiled, smoothed his mustache, and waved us over. It was like a dream come true!

The usher at the end of the aisle stopped us as we headed toward the field, but those magical yellow passes did the trick. Famosa helped each of us clear the fence and hop onto the dirt track of the field.

"Whoa!" Mike said. "This is awesome."

It really did feel awesome to be *on* the field. We walked toward the dugout. Arnie Mickel, the announcer, was standing nearby. He was holding a microphone and appeared to be getting ready to film something for the game. "Hey, Mick," I said, as casually as I could.

"Hey, kid," he said. Then, watching us head toward the dugout, he yelled, "What the heck? They don't even let *us* in the dugout before the game."

I laughed and tried to take it all in. The ballpark felt bigger than it ever had. And the ball moved so much faster. Even the slow batting-practice pitches seemed to be whizzing in at ninety miles an hour. And when the ball was hit, it flew like a bullet out of a rifle. The powerful hitter Rafael Boyar was taking his practice swings, hammering the ball into the seats. He was supposedly still recovering from an injury, but he looked pretty strong to me.

Famosa gestured toward the dugout, indicating that we should come in. It was almost scary, being so close to the players I had spent so much time admiring from afar. I couldn't think what to say to any of them. I just nodded and smiled. Mostly, they ignored us.

"What are we doing?" I muttered to Maria.

"Looking for clues," she said. "Check out everything." It was then that I noticed her spy camera, peeking out of her pocket. She was secretly recording everything in the dugout, collecting footage we could examine later. "And make note of everyone who has access to this dugout. That's our suspect list."

But they were mostly just players. A few other guys I didn't recognize. Maybe the trainer. Could he be a suspect? He seemed innocent enough, but what did I know? Mike didn't seem to be worried about searching for clues. He was chatting with all the players and getting them to sign a ball. I couldn't believe it! I had forgotten to even bring anything for an autograph! Each guy signed it and passed it to the next guy. Some of them were stretching, some were just relaxing. Some were getting ready to take their turn at batting practice. It seemed like a pretty fun life.

Before long, Famosa whispered something to Maria in Spanish, and she shot something back. He said it again. Maria sighed.

"He says we have to go," she said.

"Do you think we got what we need?" I asked.

"I do!" Mike said, admiring the ball.

"I think so," Maria said, patting the spy camera. "I'll watch this tonight."

CHAPTER TWENTY-TWO

Maria's spy camera had an attachment she could snap on that allowed her to watch the footage without having to hook it up to a computer. She spent the next hour staring into the eyepiece. I was getting bored waiting for the game to start and had already eaten a cheesesteak, so I kept pestering her.

"See anything?"

"No!"

"See anything?"

"No!"

"See anything?"

"I'll let you know when I do!"

She never let me know. The footage was useless. The game was a letdown. I won't say much about who won other than that Dad was the only happy person in the car on the way back.

We headed home feeling bummed. Being in the dugout was cool. And the ballpark is always great. But it was a fairly disappointing night. The Phils lost. No clues were found. It was a waste of time. Judging from the silence in the car, I wasn't the only one feeling down.

Dad jumped in, trying to cheer us up. "I think what we need is a more scientific method," he said. We groaned. "Hear me out! You've been running around, chasing every suspect you can think of. If you're trying to start at fifty thousand people and narrow it down one by one, you'll never solve this. You need to start with a list of zero and add suspects. Then take that small list and cross everyone off one by one."

"That's what we've been doing!" I said.

"Well, who have you crossed off?" he said.

"You, first of all," Mike said. Dad laughed. "And Famosa. Plus, all the players who were on the field at the time. Lenny said RJ was fine before the game, so we're thinking this had to happen *during* the game. Remember how the trainer took RJ a drink? It caught my eye. I'd never seen that before. The poison had to be in the water bottle! So the person who poisoned RJ had to be in the dugout!"

"That would be just a few substitute players, the manager and coaches . . . ," I said.

"Rafael Boyar was in the dugout," Maria said. "I'm always bummed when he's not in the lineup. But why would he want to hurt RJ? No one in that dugout had anything like a motive," Maria said.

The discussion went on like this for a while, getting nowhere. We reached Mike's house first, and Dad pulled into his driveway to drop him off. Mike hopped out of the car, then stopped and looked back. He gestured for me to roll down the window.

"Here, Lenny," Mike said. "I want to give this to you for your collection." He tossed me the ball he'd gotten all the guys to autograph. I dropped it. It rolled onto the seat of the car.

"Nah, Mike," I said. "You keep this one. I owe you."

"Excuse me!" Maria said. "Who set this whole thing up?!"

"Yeah!" Other Mike said. "And don't forget who made the 'for the honor of Mizlon' speech back at the mall."

"Oh, you don't want the ball anyway," Mike said. "And, Maria—don't you think Lenny deserves it? He was so close to his dream of being an announcer, only to have it slip away. That's gotta hurt."

"Yeah, you're right," she said. "But don't think I'm giving Lenny a birthday gift. Too bad. I had the perfect present in mind: a stuffed groundhog."

"Ha-ha. Very funny," I said.

"One more question, Dr. Norbeck," Mike said, leaning into the car window from the dark driveway. "Forget motive for a second. Let's forget *why* and focus on *how*. Serious question: is there anything that could be slipped into someone's drink to make them die like RJ did? Forget whether it's likely or not. Just is there a pill or something they could give a person that could make an otherwise healthy guy have a heart attack?"

"It's unlikely," Dad said. "But maybe some heart medicine, used incorrectly. It would be hard to come by, though."

"Hard, but not impossible, right?" I said.

"Right," he said. "But pretty hard. Unless you had a prescription."

CHAPTER TWENTY-THREE

Hearing Dad say what he did about heart medicine caused a major click in my brain. Not just a click, a loud *thwack*, like a fastball getting mashed by a slugger. Solving a mystery was just like understanding a baseball play. Follow the ball. Third base to second base to first base. One, two, three. It was as clear to me as a line drive to the forehead. You're out. Now it was just a matter of applying the tag. I had been thinking about it all night, piecing clues together, going over everything. Who had access to the dugout? Who had access to heart medicine? Who had a reason to want Weathers dead?

Okay, it wasn't quite that simple. I spent most of the night arguing with myself. "Could it be? No, it couldn't. But maybe? Yes! It has to be! Does it?" Yes, both halves of that conversation were me. It's bad enough to talk to yourself, but really worrisome when you start to answer. I couldn't get it out of my mind, though. Even my dreams returned to the question, waking me up to debate it over and over again. Finally, I just got up and watched the clock, waiting for it to be no longer too early to call Mike. I broke down at about eight o'clock.

"I know who did it," I said to him on the phone first thing in the morning. "And I know why."

"Who is this?" Mike said.

From those words, it was a short trip to where this tale began: me and the Mikes, crouched behind a dirty shed, waiting to die. It was a pretty dumb idea to go out there to the murderer's house on our own. I know it was. Believe me, I know. We should have asked an adult. We should have called the police. We should have at least asked Maria—who was, quite honestly, the toughest of the four of us—to go along. We should have done a million different things. But we went for it alone. Just me and the boys. Just Lenny and the Mikes.

I didn't even know what I thought we'd find. A final clue? Proof? I thought we needed one more thing to seal the case tight. So we rode our bikes out to the weird part of town, where everything is wilting and worn. It was a long ride, and even though we were excited, we took our time. We rode slowly, like cowboys coming home after a long day on the range. No one made jokes about our fake biker gang. No one joked about anything. We hardly talked at all. Once we had the place in sight, we parked our bikes and went the final few hundred yards on foot.

As we walked, we began to talk. I started, "Think about when it happened. RJ had given up eight runs in the first inning. Just one out. His ERA was two hundred and sixteen. A record. The worst of all time." I was getting excited, walking faster, making circles around the Mikes. "I know what that feels like. To be the worst ever. It's a terrible feeling. You'd want to end it any way you could."

"Are you saying—?" Mike asked.

"Right. At the exact moment that RJ's ERA became the worst in history, the *former* record holder had a chance to make sure it would stay there always. If RJ pitched another day—even recorded *one more out*—he would not go down in history as the worst ever. And he was young. He had a whole career ahead of him. He wasn't going to pitch in only one game. He wasn't going to get shipped off to war."

"Are you saying—?" both Mikes asked this time.

"Yes. The man whose name would be erased from the record books was standing right there in the dugout, armed with a deadly drug. Blaze O'Farrell killed R. J. Weathers."

"I see he had a motive. That sounds like a pretty reasonable 'why.' Nobody wants to go down in history as the worst ever at something."

"You're telling me," I said. All along I had been saying I was the worst ever, but really I wasn't.

"But *how?*" Mike asked. "How could he slip the poison into RJ's drink?"

"That's easy, sports fans," I said. "The hidden-ball trick."

They nodded. It made sense. Blaze was in the dugout the night RJ died. He had the poison on him. And he was a master at deception. Maybe he already had the medicine with him and sensed an opportunity too good to pass up. An opportunity to get his name removed from the record books. He had to be the guy.

"What are we going to do?" Other Mike asked

as we got close. "Knock on the door and tell him we're here to make a citizen's arrest?"

"No, we're just looking for clues," I said.

"Clues like what?" Mike asked.

"Remember when we thought we found stuff to make a bomb? I don't think it was for bomb making. I think it was heart medicine. And my dad said that heart medicine could be used to kill someone and make it look like a heart attack!"

"To the garbage barrel! That's where we saw the nitro-whatever."

"To the garbage barrel!" Other Mike said, giggling. It *was* sort of funny.

We stealthily made our way around Blaze's property, searching for the vial that might have killed R. J. Weathers. We found the garbage barrel and lifted the lid. It smelled awful. Like a used diaper wrapped in roadkill. And left to rot in the sun. Why did it have to be so hot?

I dug through the black garbage-y sludge and found a small bottle just like the one we had found last time we were here. I was able to wipe off the stink and hold the bottle close enough to read the smeared lettering. It was a challenge to hold it that close without throwing up, but I did it. Nitroglycerin. *Boom.*

"We got what we need," I said. "Now let's get—"

And that's when we heard the sound of breaking glass. Bottles, raining down on us. Again. Mike picked up the lid of the trash can and used it to block the bottles. Each one, chucked at major league speed, was blocked easily. He was like a knight wielding a shield. No, he was like a catcher blocking wild pitches. Wherever the throw was, he countered it easily.

"If we get out of this alive," I said, "you really should try out for catcher. You have my support. One hundred percent."

"Thanks, Len."

The bottles kept pouring down. Blaze must really have drunk a lot. Or never taken out the garbage. Or both.

This was getting old. Blaze must have thought so too. Because he took it to the next level.

"Time to end this!" he shouted. Uh-oh.

"End this? What does that mean?" Other Mike asked quietly.

"Time to end yooooooooou!"

I didn't like the sound of that.

And that, sports fans, is exactly where we started this tale. There were prayers. There were promises. There were tears. There were three friends who just wanted summer to be fun. There were three friends who just wanted to have justice done. There were three friends who just did not want to die.

And then we heard it. A blast shattering the air. Too loud to be a gun. It had to be a bomb. Could it be?

It was quiet for a minute. Maybe more. Who could tell? The next thing we heard was a confusing sound. A shouted voice, somewhat recognizable, cutting through the silence.

"I am armed and I know how to use it," the voice said. It seemed to be coming from the driveway.

"Dude, what is going on?" I asked Other Mike.

"Is that Courtney?" Mike said.

"I think it is!" I said, peeking out from behind the trash can. "She doesn't really have a gun, does she?"

"I think that noise was just her car backfiring!" Other Mike said.

"But Blaze does have a gun!" I yelled. "Courtney, look out!"

Blaze came at Courtney, raising his gun and pointing it shakily at her. He glanced at us over by the trash cans. He looked confused. I felt confused, too. And scared. He closed one eye and crouched a little, like he was going to shoot. But before he could squeeze the trigger, Courtney's right arm went back—and then Blaze went down!

She had flung something at him and nailed him right between the eyes. He was out cold. Maybe dead!

"Nah, he isn't dead," Courtney said as we rushed over to her. "At least, I don't think." She walked over to him and poked him with the toe of her sandal. She grabbed the gun and flicked the safety on. She stuck it in her purse. He groaned and coughed slightly. "See?" she said happily.

I walked over and said, "Blair O'Farrell, I am placing you under citizen's arrest for the murder of R. J. Weathers." I had no idea if that worked, but it seemed like the thing to do.

Blaze stirred again. His wrinkled face looked sad, like a baseball glove left out in the rain. "I never meant to kill him," he said quietly. "I just wanted to end his career. I couldn't resist it. So many years I lived with the shame. The worst pitcher ever. Ever! In the whole history. Of all Major League Baseball. Me." He spoke in short, sobbing bursts, taking breaks to honk his nose into a

yellowed handkerchief. "To live with that every day? Every morning when you wake up, you play that same scene over and over and over again. That same awful inning. Ball four, ball four, ball four, wild pitch, home run by that godforsaken Bill Nicholson. I even walked Putsy Caballero. Stupid Putsy Caba-freaking-llero."

I stifled a chuckle. This really wasn't a time for laughter, but come on: Putsy Caballero.

Blaze continued: "And then of all the rotten luck—to get shipped off to war and never have a chance to take the mound again? Let's face it: I'm an old man. My time on this earth is short. I don't want to be remembered as the worst ever. But I never meant to kill that kid—honest. I just thought I could slip something in his drink, maybe get him pulled from the game, maybe he'd never come back, maybe he'd get sent to the minors and I could die in peace. Maybe I'd lose my place in the record books. I didn't know it would kill him. I swear."

I didn't know what to say to all this. Then Mike quietly said, "Len, you were right."

And I felt proud. I *was* right. Blaze O'Farrell had used the hidden-ball trick.

The police showed up to violently disrupt the

silence, their sirens wailing like crying babies. Their tires kicked up dirt and mighty clouds of dust. Two large officers came sprinting out of their cars.

"Let me see your hands!" one of the cops yelled, and Blaze didn't put up a fight. The other snapped on the handcuffs and the first stayed to talk to Courtney. She gave him the gun from her purse. He smiled. They talked while Blaze waited in the police car, stuck in the back like a kid. And before long they were gone.

"I'm still a little confused about one thing," I said.

"You're confused about a lot of things, Lenny," Courtney said. "Believe me."

"Ha . . . ha," I said. "But what the heck? You really were armed? What did you hit him with?"

She showed me the device. I had no idea what I was looking at.

"It's like a homemade blackjack," she said. "You know, like the old rock in a sock."

"What? What's it made out of?" I was impressed.

"Easy," she said. "I grabbed a baseball from your room and stuck it in a bikini top. Makes a pretty awesome weapon. I like to stock up."

"Unbelievable," I said.

The Mikes echoed me. *"Unbelievable."*

Courtney smiled and shrugged. "The ball had a bunch of writing on it, so I washed it off."

"What!?" I yelled. "The autographs!"

"Kidding, Len, kidding," she said with a smile. "It's just an old ball. You need to relax, really."

"You're insane, you know that?" I asked.

"No, I'm just very savvy," she said. "I'm actually trained in the martial arts. I've been watching you like a hawk all summer, you just haven't realized it. I'm here to protect you. Why do you think your parents hired me, Lenny? My height? My hair? My tan?"

I didn't know what to say to that.

"I have a question: how did you find us?" Other Mike asked.

"Easy," she said. "Lenny's phone has GPS tracking. I've been watching you guys pretty much all summer."

"It does?" Other Mike asked. "Hey, Len, I *told* you I had the feeling we were being watched all summer!" He looked triumphant, then suddenly sad. "Man, I thought I was going to invent the bike GPS. No one is going to buy a bike GPS if phones already have one."

"Time for a new dream, warlock," she said, ruffling his hair. He laughed. We all laughed. It was a weird moment, and we didn't know what else to do but laugh. Blaze was no doubt headed to jail. I was no doubt headed to being grounded. Courtney was no doubt headed to a bright career as a CIA agent or a ninja. Mike was no doubt getting back on the baseball team—behind the plate instead of on the mound. He was going to be great. Other Mike was most certainly *not* heading downtown to give away his computer to poor children. Mike's sister, Arianna, should not hold her breath waiting for her brother to start being nice to her.

And that'll do it from Schwenkfelder, sports fans. It shaped up to be a real wild one, and the result was in doubt right up until the last pitch was thrown. But thanks to some razzle-dazzle and a solid team effort, the good guys came away with the victory. Ain't that swell?